Tales the Moon Told Me

Alyx Jae Shaw

Published by Arian Derwydd Books, LLC, 2024

Join Alyx Jae Shaw and her motley crew of characters as she draws open the curtains, giving readers a glimpse into the scenes of various lives and loves — read as they venture through tumultuous romances, titillating scenarios, and lovely poems.

Chapter 1: Saving Lazlo

Seth sighed as he slowed for a red light and felt that oh-so-telling shudder that meant the car was stalling again. Just one more problem in a long litany of troubles, all of which could be spelled M-O-N-E-Y. Beside him, his sister Jenny laughed and clapped her hands. He gave her a weary grin.

"Well, at least someone is amused," he muttered.

She laughed again, and he smiled, then heaved a sigh of relief as the sickly vehicle coughed into life, this time before he received the official city car horn salute. The light turned green, and they started forward.

"We're almost to the park," he said.

Jenny stared forward, saying nothing. That was another concern, the way she had ceased to speak more than the occasional word since their parents had died. But he was determined that today he and Jenny were going to have a nice afternoon. No worrying about the lack of funds, no fretting about her disability, just a nice day outside. He wasn't even going to worry about the way she would periodically yell… "Azwo!"

… that.

"Jenny, what is an azwo?"

"Azwo!"

"Yes, but what *is* it?"

"Azwo!" She bounced in her seat and clapped her hands.

Seth shrugged. "Well, whatever it is, you seen darn happy about it."

"Azwo," she repeated and laughed.

Seth rolled his eyes. "Fine, 'azwo' to you, too."

He pulled into the small parking lot and ground his teeth when he saw two of the three handicapped spaces were taken up by an SUV full of teenagers. He growled, fighting an urge to get out of his car with a baseball bat and start smashing heads. The attitudes and excuses he had encountered over the years gave him a rabid hate of people who used handicap parking spots without regard for those who needed them, and he had heard every excuse in the book, from "I was just going to be here a second" to "well, just how many handicapped people are supposed to be out today anyway?"

What, was there a rule he didn't know about? Were there days when persons with disabilities were supposed to stay home and put their lives on hold so soccer moms, who thought their crap smelled like roses, could use up spaces they weren't entitled to so they wouldn't have to jar the heels of their Italian leather shoes walking across the fucking parking lot?

"Calm down, Seth," he said to himself. "Just breathe, this is supposed to be a nice day, nice family outing, you and Jenny at the park to watch the birdies and smell the flowers. Don't let them bother you..."

He parked in the third space and opened the door. He walked around to the back of the over-worked van and opened the hatch to pull out the wheelchair. One of the teenagers raised his head, some little reverse-Oreo gangsta wanna-be who would probably piss himself in terror and submission if the real thing so much as sneezed in his general direction.

"Yo dog, not so close to the ride."

Seth paused and slowly swung his head to look at the scrawny little bent-neck ass wipe in his shit-catcher pants and fake 'bling,' He ground his teeth with the sort of rage that can only come of a very long, hard week, too much stress, and the final straw. His eye twitched.

"How about your move your piece of shit car so I don't cram this wheelchair up your ass, rip your head off, and fuck the bleeding stump?"

The teenager was taken aback. "Harsh, man."

"Push me, Vanilla Ice. I fucking dare you."

"Yo, you are one cold dude."

"Then stay out of my parking spot."

Seth managed to get Jenny's wheelchair out of the car and opened up, but she didn't want to use it. So he followed after her with it as she made her slow and determined way across the lawn to a flowering bush, knowing she would need it soon enough. She could walk, but she was weak, having the narrow airways in her lungs that plagued many who had Down's syndrome, and lengthy strolls were not her cup of tea. She made it to the bush and sat down gracelessly on the grass to admire the white flowers, happy just to watch and smell them. She was wearing her favourite blue dress, her dark hair up in ribbons, and she smiled at the way the light shone down on the green leaves and soft blossoms. Seth envied her the simple joy. His own guts were filled with ulcers from strain and worry, and if he did not sell one of his custom-built motorcycles soon, then he did not know what they would do. They might even have to sell their house.

"Azwo!"

Seth jumped, startled from his worries by the cry. He looked over at his sister. "Jenny, please, just tell me what on earth is an azwo?"

"Azwo!" she shouted happily, and Seth gasped as he heard an answering cry.

"Jenny! How's my beautiful girl?"

Seth's head snapped in the direction of the response, and he saw a man walking towards his sister. He felt his hackles rise almost instinctively, wanting to protect his helpless sibling, but Jenny did not seem to feel she needed protecting. She held her arms out to the stranger, who was clearly not unknown to her, and they hugged. He was rather short, with tanned skin and long dark brown hair tied back into a messy ponytail. His nearly-black eyes were shaded by a pair of pink-tinted granny style glasses that had long gone out of fashion for everyone save diehard John Lennon fans. Over his purple T-shirt with its dancing daisy motif, worn jeans, and sandals, he had a white lab coat. Seth watched as he seated himself on the grass, and Jenny reached into one of the coat's pockets for a soft caramel.

"So," said Seth, "I'm not the only man in Jenny's life."

"Nope," said the stranger. "Me and Jenny are going to get married some day. Aren't we, sweetie?" The man glanced up at Seth. "I'm Lazlo."

Seth grinned as realization sank in. "Azwo."

"Well, that is my secret identity, known only to my best friends. Are you Jenny's new caregiver?"

"No, I'm her brother, Seth. I am so glad to meet you. She really had me going. Every time we drive by this park, she yells 'Azwo! Azwo!' I had no idea what she was on about."

"Oh, I work at the building across the street," he said, gesturing at an imposing white structure. "I come here to eat lunch and stare at something that's not waving tail spikes at me from a slide beneath a microscope. Personally, I'm certain the little buggers are giving me the finger."

Seth laughed. "Could be a lewd invitation."

Lazlo grinned. "Hope not. Some of these little guys can do ugly, ugly things to a person." He smiled as Jenny fished another caramel out of his pocket.

Seth sat down on the grass with them. "So how did you and Jenny meet?"

"Oh, she was here with her caretaker. She just toddled right over to me and sat down and delighted me with her insight about the political structure in Russia during the time of Stalin. Then she stole all my caramels, and we've been pals ever since." He grinned. "I was getting a little concerned about her. I hadn't seen her in a few days."

"Yeah, well, I had to let her caretaker go, and we haven't had much time," said Seth. He did not mention having to close down his shop and move his business into his garage in order to be able to afford to eat. He felt his ulcer mumble angrily in his belly. He winced slightly but forced himself to ignore it. If Lazlo noticed, he said nothing.

"There you are!" called a voice, and Lazlo looked up.

Seth, too, raised his head and watched as a beautiful woman crossed the grass towards them. Her clothing was more conservative than Lazlo's, but even without the white coat, Seth had the impression she was a coworker of his. She walked up to Lazlo and stared down at him, her long reddish hair tied back from her face.

"If you were going to hide from me, then you should have picked a bigger bush."

"We picked the one with the cloaking device, but it's not working today." Lazlo rose to his feet. "Beth, Seth. Seth, Beth. Hey, you rhyme."

The woman rolled her eyes and smiled. "Pleased to meet you."

Seth was normally a rather shy individual and approaching women was not his most shining social ability. He fully succeeded in horrifying himself by opening his mouth and saying, "Hello, nurse!"

Beth's smile became rather plastic. "*Doctor*, actually," she said coolly and crossed her arms over a pair of breasts that infants saw in their dreams. "I was considering doing a paper on Neanderthal man. Perhaps you'd like to volunteer as a test subject?"

Seth sighed, feeling his cheeks burn, and he stepped back a pace, his natural shyness coming over him like a blanket. He shoved his black hair back with a hand stained by engine grease.

"No," he muttered, "I'm not that advanced. I'm still trying to master walking upright. Sorry."

Beth's smile because more natural, and she seemed to decide to take the faux pas for what it was: an unintentional slip and an attempt at a compliment. "So you are our Jenny's new caregiver?"

"No, big brother. I didn't realize she ran with such a distinguished crowd. So you are a scientist, too?"

"Scientific researcher, working with viruses and infectious diseases, yes. What field are you in?"

"The back lot. I'm not any sort of scientist." He reached for his wallet and pulled out of it a handful of photographs of bikes he had built. "Seth make shiny things go fast."

"A noble pursuit," said Beth. She took the pictures and looked at the motorcycles. "These are gorgeous. They ought to be in a museum. You make these?"

Seth nodded. "Yeah. I design them and make them. I have… had… a small shop."

"What happened to it?" asked Beth.

Seth didn't really want to say. He didn't like the idea of spewing his troubles to a stranger. He gave her the abridged version.

"Well, I just… I just buried my dad, and then Jenny needed some things. I had to cancel orders, and… well, I guess you could say death by circumstance."

"This black and silver bike is… sooooooo lovely. Looks fragile, though."

"Yeah, I know, I created it to look that way, but if you look here… and… here… and this bit here… it's actually heavily reinforced. I mean, I wouldn't take it off-roading, but for a fly ride in the summer, he wouldn't let you down."

Beth laughed. "He? I thought all machines were female."

Seth shrugged. "Alley Cat's a boy. He told me."

"Alley Cat. That's cute. Maybe I should come over and ask him if he wants to come home with me." Beth looked concerned as she studied the picture of the black motorcycle. "Probably expensive, isn't it?"

"Well… it is a custom-made, one-of-a-kind bike. It's like art you can ride."

"It's so elegant. My boyfriend would flip. Can I come by tomorrow and look at the bike?"

Seth mentally did a dance. "Absolutely." He took out a business card and wrote his home address on the back. "I'm working out of my garage now. Business hours are still the same."

"Great!" Beth accepted the card, then looked around, noticing Lazlo and Jenny seemed to have wandered off. "Now where did Lazlo escape to? Ah. There he is." She rolled her eyes as she saw him sitting on the grass with Jenny. They were eating ice cream, and Jenny was putting flowers in his unruly hair. She sighed. "Great. We have the head of the department coming by this afternoon, and our top research scientist is covered in grass stains, flowers, and ice cream. Not exactly confidence-inspiring."

Seth grinned. "Is he your boyfriend?"

"Lazlo? I wish. I'd take the little darling home in a heartbeat. But he's involved already, and even if he wasn't, I'm not exactly built according to his tastes."

Seth blinked. "But you're beautiful. What could he possibly want to change?"

"Well, that's what I keep asking myself, but Lazlo is a jerk. He insists on liking guys."

Seth's gaze snapped towards the man sitting with his sister, grass and dandelions in his hair. "He's gay?"

"Do you have a problem with that?"

"No, I just… picture gay guys as neat and well dressed and clean."

Beth patted him on the shoulder. "I'm sorry, Seth. The media lied to you. This one washes his dishes by licking them and considers pork rinds a condiment."

"You mean they're not?"

Beth rolled her eyes and laughed. "God, not another one."

They went to where Lazlo and Jenny were sitting, and as they drew near, Seth drew a quiet gasp of utter astonishment. He stopped and stared, jaw hanging in utter astonishment. Talking. Jenny was talking. She'd hardly said a word in ages, but here she was chatting. Seth felt his knees start to collapse, and he put a hand out, feeling Beth catch him and lower him slowly to the grass.

"Seth, are you all right?"

"She's talking!"

"Of course, she's talking. She and Lazlo chat all the time!"

Seth shook his head. "She's hardly said a thing since Dad died! I've been worried sick! I've been going out of my mind trying to figure out what she wants and needs and how she's feeling, and…"

Seth watched as his sister held a simple conversation about dandelions with Lazlo. Finally, he managed to get to his feet and walked over to the pair, astonished. He sank down to the grass beside Lazlo, green eyes large.

"You spoke!" he said to Jenny.

Jenny smiled but said nothing. Seth turned his head to look at Lazlo.

"How did you get her to do that?"

Lazlo blinked. "I gather she doesn't talk to you."

"No, and it's been making me crazy! Trying to figure out what she wants, what she needs, how she feels…"

"Well, seems to me Jenny has figured out she doesn't have to talk. She can just sit back and watch you go crazy. It's probably a lot more fun than just telling you what she needs."

Seth shook his head, it having never occurred to him that Jenny might simply not need to tell him anything.

"Jenny?" he asked, his voice full of astonishment. "Did you play a trick on me?"

Found out at last, Jenny laughed and clapped her hands. "I did!"

* * *

It was the start of a beautiful friendship.

Beth bought the bike, much to her boyfriend Victor's complete dismay. He remained highly displeased until Beth sent him a picture of the elegant, low-slung machine, then ordered one for himself that matched. It was a very welcome and desperately needed cash infusion, and at long last, Seth felt the pain in his guts relent. He traded in his old battered van for a newer and more reliable one, caught up on his bills, and once more began making motorcycles. This time, he did not invest in a shop; he continued to work in his garage. For now, he had chosen to be cautious, only spending what he had to. He was not anxious to end up in the same situation he had just climbed out of.

He took Jenny to the park daily, always in time to meet up with Beth and Lazlo. On days when the weather was unpleasant, they would meet in the coffee shop near the park. Eventually, Beth and Lazlo became regular visitors to Seth and Jenny's house. Lazlo especially would often pop by, usually with some small gift for Jenny. Seth still felt a little protective towards her, but there was little doubt Lazlo's presence was having a positive effect. She had almost shut out the world after their father died, his death coming too close after their mother's, and it had been an enormous strain on both of them.

Now that she had something to look forward to, she had come out of her shell and was much more conversational. There were still problems with her lungs to deal with, the narrowed airways associated with Down's making her weak and easily tired, and there were still occasional periods of time when she would sit and stare, as if mulling the questions of the universe over in her mind. But she had always been content to sit and play by herself or stare thoughtfully.

Now she seemed more interested in life around her and more interactive, and Seth had no doubt this was largely due to Lazlo.

He did harbour a secret suspicion that Lazlo was possibly using Jenny as something of a guinea pig. A few of the toys he brought for her were, without question, prototypes designed to help build brain function. Since much of the research Lazlo had once been involved with had to do with how illness and disability affected the way the brain worked, Seth knew the elaborate devices had to be somehow connected with it. However, he was not about to complain. Jenny had gone from almost non-responsive to chatty and lively and was taking more of an interest in her own care. It was a huge load off Seth's shoulders.

Still, there was something a little daunting about having Lazlo as a friend. He was a nice guy, and Seth very much enjoyed his easy-natured and even goofy disposition, but his intelligence was downright daunting. He was a happy-go-lucky guy who enjoyed a cold beer on a hot day, loved learning about the motorcycles, and happened to have written papers on the mutation of DNA in viruses and could, if he felt like it, explain his hypothesis regarding how some viruses could build their own DNA inside a host cell. Seth listened to this theory as it was delivered by a guy wearing sandals, torn jeans, and a blue T-shirt with a dancing pig on it, Jenny's princess tiara perched on his head. When Lazlo was done, he smiled brightly.

"What do you think?"

Seth stared back at him blankly, blinking. "Og find food now."

Lazlo laughed. "Food good. Splog help Og."

Seth glanced at Jenny, who was having one of her thoughtful moments, holding her favourite doll, staring out the window. Lazlo set the tiara on the coffee table, and he and Seth went into the kitchen to make dinner.

"So what made you take an interest in viruses?" asked Seth.

Lazlo shrugged. "Well, I wish I had some heartrending story to tell you about how my dog Spike died of an acute attack of Necrotizing Fasciitis and how deeply it affected me, but the truth of the matter is I just think they're cool. Then I sort of went from the viruses themselves to the effect they can have on the brain and… got side-tracked. Then I found out the company I was working for wanted this information not, as I had been told, to cure these ailments, but to cultivate certain traits so they could mutate these viruses and unleash them on enemy soldiers. That was when I decided Canada sounded like a nice place to live. So I left Florida, arrived here in the middle of a blizzard, curled into a foetal position, and sucked my thumb for a while. Then a research company offered me a chance to use my expertise to see if I can mutate a virus to act as a sort of shut-off, to go in and tell a virus that is ordinarily fatal to… turn off, to stop doing what it is doing, force it into dormancy or something. Some of these little bastards are surprisingly tricky, and they change so fast that developing vaccines is nearly impossible. First, however, I have to figure out how they do what they do."

Seth shook his head. "Better you than me. I failed high school science."

"Yeah, and I can't change a flat, so we're even." Lazlo grinned. He brushed past Seth as he went to find something in the cupboard.

Seth sighed. "You're flirting."

"I'm not flirting. I'm… merely having a perfectly understandable mammalian reaction to your proximity."

"You're flirting."

"Oh, get over yourself. Where do you keep the kidney beans?"

"Kidney beans? I thought we were making spaghetti sauce."

"I thought we were making chilli."

Seth shrugged. "Okay, chilli it is."

Lazlo found the beans and let out a short shriek of delight. "Oh, isn't this just all so warm and fuzzy and domestic?"

Seth closed his eyes and mentally counted to ten. "Don't you have a boyfriend?"

"I have the most gorgeous male to ever draw breath." Lazlo pulled a handful of photos out of his wallet, showing them to Seth.

"Laird. Breathtaking, isn't he?"

"He's… a guy."

Lazlo gave Seth a jaundiced look. "You know, studies have shown that admitting another man is attractive neither makes you gay nor causes your testicles to fall off."

"Okay, fine, he's a pretty good-looking guy. So why are you up here flirting with me?"

"I wasn't flirting. But I am sure Freud would have had some theories about you assuming I was."

"Freud was a moron."

"He was," said Lazlo, "but he did have some great theories."

Seth laughed. "So is Laird a scientist, too?"

"Yeah. Well… he's… he is very good at his job."

"Which is?"

"Well, he's… actually a lab assistant. But he's very good at it."

"Must make things interesting, you at the top of your field, and him having to shovel up after you."

"Hey, he's the man I want to marry. I'd love him if he made wattle-and-daub walls for monkey houses."

Seth laughed. "And what does he think about you coming up to visit me?"

Lazlo put the photos back into his wallet, shoved it back into his pocket, then pulled out a large pot from a cupboard. "He and I are a happy and trusting couple, but socially, we are very different. Laird likes solitude. I like people. So I go out and visit people, and he sits alone and pursues his own theories. He might just be an assistant now, but one day, he will be on the same level I am."

"And he doesn't mind you flirting?"

"I was not flirting with you. If I was flirting, I would have done this."

Seth felt a hand grab his ass. He jumped, eyes large, and then spun to face Lazlo, who blinked at him innocently. Seth pointed to the kitchen door.

"Out."

Lazlo rolled his eyes. "Oh, get over yourself."

Lazlo went to sit with Jenny, while Seth continued making dinner. When everything was in order, he went into the living room but did not see Jenny and Lazlo at all. He did, however, hear noises coming from the bathroom. He closed his eyes and mentally counted to ten, then went into the bathroom. The shower was running, the floor was drenched, and he could hear what could only be described as barnyard noise and pirate-speak coming from the tub. He pulled back the curtain and looked inside. There were Jenny and Lazlo, soaking wet, wearing makeshift pirate costumes, and holding the old paddles from a small rowboat he owned. Lazlo and Jenny stared back at him. Seth crossed his arms and awaited an explanation. Lazlo blinked at him from behind his pink-tinted glasses.

"Do you mind?" said Lazlo. "You're letting all the animals out of the ark."

"If you're playing Noah's Ark, then why are you dressed as pirates?"

"Who are you, the imagination police?"

Seth rolled his eyes. "Dinner will be ready soon." He closed the shower curtain and walked away.

Lazlo and Jenny mopped up after they finally reached the end of their voyage. Seth laid out dinner, and they ate. By then, Jenny was ready for bed, and Seth helped her to get ready. When she at last was tucked in and asleep, he went into the kitchen and got a couple cans of beer for himself and Lazlo. They sat together on the couch in the living room in comfortable silence for a while.

"I really appreciate everything you have done for Jenny," said Seth quietly.

"I haven't done anything, really."

"But you have. She's so much happier, and…"

"I didn't do anything," said Lazlo. "Other than offer my friendship."

"That's something. You have no idea the way some people react to her. Like she's sub-human. Breaks my heart. She just wants what every other kid wants. I mean, okay, I know physically she's not a child, but that's what she is. And people treat her like a freak. She's just my sister, and if they bothered to get their heads out of their asses, they could see what a neat person she is!"

"My world," said Lazlo, "welcome to it."

Seth gave Lazlo a questioning glance, then realization dawned. "Because you're gay."

He shrugged. "Because of that, or because I'm not white. You'd be amazed at how many people will start bitching about how 'nonwhites' are taking over while you're right there to hear it, like they just assume you can't speak the language. I have doctorates and PhDs coming out my ears. I have an IQ of 166. I am one of the leading scientists in my field, but because I'm a funny colour, people just assume I am some uneducated immigrant living in a closet with my family of fifty. And what really burns my ass is when they see me with my tall, blonde-haired, blue-eyed boyfriend and assume *he* is the successful one, and I'm José the pool-boy."

Seth gazed at Lazlo, taking in the black eyes, near-black hair, and deeply tanned skin. "So… what are you?"

"Cuban, actually. Well, my parents are from Cuba. I was born in the States then came up here."

Seth stared at him a little while longer, then shrugged. "Well, I never noticed. I was just gonna ask you how you got your tan to last so damned long."

Lazlo raised an eyebrow in surprise. "You're kidding me."

"No. Sorry, man, I… really didn't notice you weren't white."

"How can you not notice?"

"I'm sorry. You are the same colour as every other English Bay beach bum. I mean, look at me. I have black hair. Stick me under the sun, and in a few hours, who can tell the difference? Except my eyes are green, and, once upon a time, my ancestors lived in England. Look, you like my sister, and she loves you. Frankly, that's all I give a shit about. I wouldn't care if you were orange with blue spots."

Lazlo made a face. "Well, I would. Who wants to be orange?"

"Well, if you were chartreuse, then orange might be an improvement."

"If I was chartreuse, I'd kill myself." Lazlo had a drink of beer. "Funny how some people get so worked up about crap that just shouldn't matter."

Seth gave a slight smile. "My mom used to say it was because they didn't have anything real to worry about."

"Wise woman, your mom. What did she die of?"

Seth had a swallow of beer. "She tripped, believe it or not. At the shop where she worked. Just tripped and fell and smashed her skull open on a table. Just a stupid accident. No one's fault. Then Dad had a massive stroke, which we all knew he would given the way he ate and smoked. Now it's just me and Jenny."

"No girlfriend?"

Seth shook his head. "No time. And not a lot of women want a guy with a sister who needs so much care. They don't want to end up having to help out."

"Yeah, I can see that." Lazlo smiled, his eyes becoming soft with affection. "I don't know what I would do without Laird. He's… he's my everything. I'm so crazy about him, it scares me. I just love him so much. He's so intelligent and beautiful. I love how beautiful he is."

Set smiled. "So where did you meet him?"

"He was throwing up in a garbage can outside my lab one day."

"Terrific first impression."

"Well, he certainly got my attention. Then he passed out, and… well… I'm just a sucker for a man who throws himself at my feet."

"Good grief! What was wrong with him?"

"Food poisoning. Seems the mayo in his sandwich had mutated into an alien life form. But he's better now." Lazlo grinned. "He's so cute when he's sick."

Seth chuckled. "Dude. You're hopeless."

"Yup. I've got it bad for him, no argument from me. And speaking of my darling lab-rat…" Lazlo checked his watch. "I should be off to get him. He'll be…"

Seth and Lazlo both looked up abruptly as there was a tremendous crash and then strange thumping noises. They put their beer down and ran upstairs, Seth reaching the door to Jenny's room and flinging it open. To his complete horror, she was on the floor having a violent seizure. She flopped and thumped like a broken toy, eyes rolled back in her head. Seth stared, rooted to the floor in horror, having no idea what to do. He felt Lazlo give him a slight push.

"Seth, go call an ambulance. I'll see what I can do."

* * *

There was nothing anyone could do. Seth could scarcely understand the doctor as he explained to him that Jenny had epilepsy, which had been undiagnosed. The long thoughtful silences she would experience were in fact 'absences,' a type of seizure. Then something had triggered a grand maul, a huge, violent seizure, and her weakened heart had been unable to deal with the strain. She was dead before she reached the hospital.

The days following were a blur. Seth was barely able to function, lost in grief and shock. It was Lazlo who called the funeral home and made the arrangements for a simple service, one within Seth's limited budget. It was Lazlo who helped Seth contact the friends and relatives who needed to know what had happened, helped him to deal with the forms and paperwork, and Lazlo who helped him to pick out the dress in which she would be cremated. Blue. Her favourite colour.

On the day of the viewing, Seth came in to meet with those who had gathered to say goodbye, and, though he looked for Lazlo, he did not see him. He was disappointed but not surprised. Sadly, even when one life ended, others had to go on, and Seth knew that Lazlo was working on projects that simply could not wait. Still, it angered him that Lazlo was not there. He had been so important to Jenny. Seth walked to the casket in which Jenny lay and smiled through his tears, feeling the anger melt as he saw a white lab coat folded up and placed beneath Jenny's clasped hands, the pockets filled with soft caramels. Lazlo had been unable to attend. But he had not forgotten her.

In the days that followed, Seth saw Lazlo less and less. He still met with him and Beth at the coffee shop on rainy days, and they would sit together in silence, lost in thoughts about someone who was no longer there. Seth gathered that Laird was not especially happy about Lazlo coming to visit him, and Seth could see his point. If he was in his shoes, he was pretty sure he would not like the idea of his own boyfriend going to visit a single man who lived alone. Still, it was hard. He hadn't realized that Lazlo had become as much his friend as he was Jenny's. But Laird was adamant. Bad enough Lazlo had spent so much time with Seth when Jenny was alive. He did not want him there with Seth now that she was gone.

Still, the friendship was hardly over. At least once a week, they would meet for coffee, and Beth would always call to let Seth know about any Lazlo-related news. When Beth and Victor decided to marry after eight years of living together, Beth personally invited Seth to her wedding, which meant Laird had no reason to complain about his presence.

Beth's wedding was the first time Seth actually saw Laird in the flesh, and much as his socially-ingrained distaste for admiring the beauty of other men told him not to stare, he couldn't help it. Photos simply did not do the six-foot-six ivory beauty justice. He was gorgeous, with long silvery-blonde hair that fell to the small of his back. He had long legs, a beautifully toned body, and blue-grey eyes that radiated an intense loathing for all humanity. He was as cold as he was striking.

Seth hated him almost immediately.

"I hate him," he told Lazlo as they drunkenly waltzed at the reception, Laird's eyes burning holes in Seth's flesh.

"Hate him? He's my baby! How can you…" Lazlo tripped. "…hate my baby?"

"Your baby's an asshole."

"You're straight. What do you care?"

"You're my friend. I care. Besides… he won't let you come over." Seth stumbled a little himself, the champagne wreaking havoc with his balance. "And if you don't come over, then there's no one to…" He almost said, 'paddle the Ark,' but stopped, his eyes welling with tears. He drew a steadying breath and changed the subject. "Who's leading?"

"I thought you were."

"We'll both lead."

"No, that won't work. You lead," said Lazlo. He closed his eyes and laid his head on Seth's shoulder.

Seth rolled his eyes. "Well, there goes my masculinity."

"Highly overrated and meaningless," said Lazlo.

"Well, you could at least stop stepping on my feet."

"Sorry."

They danced slowly. The evening was drawing to a close. Seth had no idea what song the band was playing, but it hardly mattered. He was gazing down at Lazlo, watching the way his shaggy dark hair hung loose and long, noticing the way the light sparkled softly on his skin. They were both covered in glitter; the whole room was, in fact. Beth's bridesmaids had been giggling and spraying each other with aerosol cans of the stuff, and there was barely a human being in the room who was not shimmering silver and pink and blue.

Seth watched the way the glitter on Lazlo's lips caught the light, and for the first time, the idea crossed his mind that he would like to kiss him. Then someone big and very blonde inserted himself abruptly between the two. Seth was nearly knocked onto his ass and was startled to find himself gazing up into blue-grey eyes. He stepped back as Lazlo was taken from him, watching as Lazlo looked up, jarred from his peacefully drunken reverie, to see Laird. He smiled and laid his head against his chest, while Laird glared hate at Seth and mouthed two words at him.

"Fuck. Off."

Seth retreated dispiritedly over to Beth and her new husband, where at least he was welcomed.

"C'mon, Seth!" said Beth, drunkenly beckoning him over. "You can s... hic! Sit with my brand-new beautiful hubby. Isn't he cute?"

Victor was big and handsome and friendly, especially tonight. He pulled Seth onto his lap and gave him a sip of his champagne, sending the bevy of drunken beauties around him into fits of giggles. Victor was not a man who minded female attention. But as Beth turned to laugh and shriek with her friends and sister, Victor lowered his head and whispered into Seth's ear.

"I hate the son of a bitch, too. You ask me, he's pure evil."

Seth turned his head, raising one eyebrow in surprise as he looked into Victor's hazel eyes. "So what did he do to you?"

"To me? Nothing. But some of Bethy's personal research went missing after Lazlo and Laird came for a visit. And Lazlo is not the sort of guy who needs to steal his research from his friends. Not with his intelligence and credentials."

"You think it was Laird?"

"I can't prove it, but yeah." Victor looked towards Lazlo and Laird as they danced, Lazlo staring up at his tall lover adoringly, his dark hair hanging over his black eyes. "Lazlo's a nice guy, and he's been one of Bethy's best friends for ages, but he's always been kinda sheltered. He was schooled at home, awarded scholarships by people who coveted his genius… he's never been hurt. He thinks Laird is protecting him, and he's not. He's using him. So… don't stop being his friend, okay? Eventually, Lazlo is gonna find out he's in love with a world class son of a bitch."

Seth looked from Victor, to Lazlo, and back again. Slowly, a thought occurred to his drunken brain.

"Lazlo's helped you in the past, too, hasn't he?"

Victor nodded. "Yeah, he did. He gave Bethy and I some money when we were in pretty desperate straits. I don't want to get into detail; it's a pretty personal matter, but… yeah. And I know of a few other people he's bailed out. Good old Lazlo, off saving the world." Victor narrowed his eyes and reached for a fresh glass of champagne, gazing at the two men dancing across the floor. "You have to ask yourself who is saving Lazlo."

* * *

Seth was not surprised that he didn't see Lazlo after the wedding. He was not at the park, and he was not at the coffee shop on rainy days. Seth tried calling his cell phone but learned his number was now blocked. The message was very clear: Laird did not want Seth anywhere near Lazlo. Still, Seth found himself going to the coffee shop, seeking out the last vestiges of the time when Jenny was alive and he was happy, but Lazlo, it seemed, had been effectively removed from his life.

"Son of a bitch," said Beth quietly, pouring sugar into her coffee. "He's got Lazlo right where he wants him. I hardly even see him myself anymore."

Seth picked at his cruller. "He called me once. I wasn't home. I tried to call back, but I got Laird."

"Yeah, Lazlo doesn't answer the phone anymore," said Beth. She sighed. "I don't know why Lazlo doesn't see what a total prick Laird is, but he doesn't. How long since you talked to Laz?"

Seth toyed with the spoon in his coffee. "Since your wedding. Seven months."

Beth gave him a sympathetic look. "How are you holding up?"

"I'm fine, I guess. Mostly I just design my bikes and work on them. Trying to save up for a larger workspace. I'm going to go camping this weekend. Try to clear my head, make a few decisions about where to go from here now that I'm all on my own."

Beth smiled. "Victor and I are going to go to Toronto in the morning and visit his mom for a few days. Lazlo's in Florida visiting his brother."

Seth snorted. "I'm surprised Laird let him go."

"Yeah, me, too. He'll be back sometime early tomorrow." Beth narrowed her eyes. "Y'know, this is bullshit. Lazlo's our friend. How about you pop by here next Thursday after I get back from Toronto, and I'll drag Laz down here for a visit? I know he misses you. He asks me about you."

Seth perked up. "Really? He does?"

She nodded. "Yeah. So screw Laird. Just because Lazlo has no idea he's in love with a bastard doesn't mean we can't see him. You in?"

Seth snorted with amusement. "Sure, why not? How often do I get a chance to help a beautiful woman kidnap a guy who researches viruses? Add a few explosions, and we can make a movie out of it."

Beth laughed, then looked at her watch. "Well, I have to get back to the germ farm." She leaned forward and gave him a kiss. "See you next week. Have fun playing with poison ivy in the woods."

"Yeah, have fun in the wilds of Toronto."

She gave him a hug and then left. Seth finished his cruller, and then he, too, left the small café. He went home and packed for his camping trip, then cleaned up the house. Satisfied all was ready, he went to bed, looking forward to a weekend alone in the woods. At five in the morning, Beth called.

* * *

Seth pulled up in front of the small cabin, cutting off the car engine and feeling a nervous tension in his guts. He stepped out of the vehicle and, felt the warmth of the summer sun on his shoulders, and heard the soft crunch of gravel and old pine cones beneath his feet. He slammed the door shut and walked towards the figure seated on the rustic steps, eyes fixed ahead at a point Seth could not see, his fingers linked loosely and resting on one knee, which was quietly vibrating. Lazlo's hair was loose and unkempt, and the eyes behind the pink lenses of his glasses were glazed and dark-rimmed. It was clear he had not slept recently.

Seth walked over to Lazlo and eased himself down beside him, reluctant to make any sudden moves or loud sounds near the badly strained man.

"Lazlo?" he said softly.

Lazlo said nothing, responding in no way to Seth's voice. Seth tried again.

"How are you?" he asked, knowing it was a stupid question but not sure what else to say to a man who was clearly in the throes of some sort of emotional meltdown, if not a full-blown nervous breakdown.

Lazlo did not respond at first, but then he replied in a tight voice, painted with hysteria.

"I wanted to come see you, but I couldn't remember your phone number, and then I came out here, and I... couldn't find my car, so I sat down, but... I'm not sure I can get back up."

"Do you want me to help you inside?"

"Not right yet." Lazlo's eyes darted nervously around the small yard, not looking at Seth. "I... I just need a minute."

Seth was no doctor, but he could tell Lazlo needed a lot more than a minute. He might even need a few days in the psychiatric wing of a hospital.

"Okay, we can just sit here for a while."

Lazlo nodded, eyes staring forward, hands on his knee, which continued its rapid bobbling. For a while, the only sound other than that of birds and squirrels was the drum of Lazlo's leather sandal hitting the step. Suddenly, he drew in a loud gasp.

"He took everything, Seth. *Everything*. The food, the furniture, the bedding, the dried flower Jenny gave me... I don't even have a chair. He took my research. All of it. Books, notes, computers... it was something I was working on in secret with my own time and resources. I have no way of proving it was mine. Gone. He emptied the bank account. He even tried to sell the house, but it was in my name." He drew in a sobbing breath and looked at Seth with eyes brimming with tears and agony. "I loved him! Why would he do that to me? I loved him, I practically worshipped him, I shared every last detail of my life with him, and I come back from a lousy three-day visit with my brother in Florida to this?"

"You didn't know he was planning on leaving?" asked Seth quietly.

"No! I had no clue! He kissed me goodbye and told me he loved me and to hurry back!" Lazlo drew in a ragged breath, his voice rising in pitch, his words tumbling out in a babble. "We were talking marriage and adoption and schools. One of the main reasons I came to Canada was I could get married. Seth, I'm really not sure I'm going to survive this. I think I'm dying..."

Seth pulled him into his arms, holding him tightly. "No, you're not," he said gently. "I won't let you. I'm here. It's okay." He rocked him gently, closing his eyes. "We'll get you calmed down, then we can go into town and..."

"No, I want to stay here. If I go into town, I'll probably come back and find my cabin on fire, and he is *not* getting my cabin."

Seth wondered if Laird actually had the guts to return to the scene of his crime but understood Lazlo's feelings on the matter. "Okay. I've got my camping stuff with me. I've got foam mattresses and sleeping bags and food and a cooler full of beer. We can have an indoor camp out."

"Fine. Sounds like fun."

Seth did not like the tone of Lazlo's voice. He was hysterical and likely exhausted as well. He needed to calm him down enough to sleep and start healing.

"Are you hungry?" Seth asked.

"No, I… I just…"

The voice trailed off, and Seth understood. He just needed to be held, to feel secure. Seth closed his eyes and held his friend tightly, stroking his hand over Lazlo's back as if he were an over-wrought toddler. Seth was almost relieved when Lazlo drew a loud gasp and broke down, crying as only one can with a truly shattered heart. He felt his eyes grow hot and wet as he recalled his own past heartbreaks.

"It's okay, Lazlo. I'm here. I'm always gonna be here."

It took some time, but eventually Seth had Lazlo settled near the fireplace inside the little cabin. He had made up a bed with two sleeping bags and a pillow on a foam mattress, gave him a can of beer, and together the pair sat, drinking beer and toasting hot dogs and marshmallows in the empty cabin.

It was not the camping trip Seth had envisioned.

Lazlo remained somewhat bewildered, but, gradually, he seemed to be recovering. He was more lucid than he had been earlier, but even Seth could tell it would be weeks, possibly months, before Lazlo was well. Something had clearly broken inside the man's head, and Seth was not letting him out of his sight.

"Your hot dog is burning," said Seth quietly.

"I know. I like them burned."

Seth smiled. "Yeah, they're good a little burned." He glanced at Lazlo. "You must be exhausted."

"I am," said Lazlo quietly. "But I don't want to sleep. I know the moment I lay down, I'll just get upset. I don't need to be upset."

"Well, what if I slept beside you?"

Lazlo shook his head. "No, a straight guy and a gay guy in the same bed is never a wise idea. For one thing, the gay guy in this particular case happens to snore like an outboard motor when he's upset, which he most certainly is. He's also a notorious spooner."

Seth grinned. "I think my masculinity can handle it. Besides, I want to. Hell, after all you did for me and Jenny, it's the least I can do." He looked at Lazlo, eyes warm. "I saw what you did."

Lazlo smiled faintly and made an attempt at humour. "Sorry, I really should have gone behind a bush."

Seth laughed. "No, I meant the coat. It was a really sweet gesture."

"A futile one. Like most gestures."

"No," said Seth quietly. "No, it wasn't. She adored you. Maybe you couldn't give her more years, but you enabled her to enjoy the time she had. You were a good friend to her and to me. And I'm glad to be here. And if you want to pass out and spoon me off the bed and mumble naughty things in your sleep about Orlando Bloom, then, by all means, go right ahead."

"Oh, I never dream about The Blooming One. I go for scruffy intellectual types."

"Interesting. So you are the man you want to sleep with."

"And I get to have me every night." Lazlo grinned briefly, but then the smile fell from his face, and his hands began to shake. Carefully, slowly, he put his rather crispy hot dog on a bun.

Seth watched, feeling a pain in his guts as this beautiful, brilliant, and loving man tried to remember how to put relish on it. "Maybe I should take you to a hospital," he said quietly, but Lazlo shook his head.

"No. What will they do? They'll put me in a room and give me drugs and stare at me to see if I turn into Renfield. I'd rather be home."

"Okay," said Seth. "But I'm staying until I'm absolutely certain you are all right."

"Then you are going to be here a long time. Look, Seth, I'm fine, really. I'm… okay…"

Seth watched Lazlo try to sort the mechanics of setting the bun down to pick up and open the relish jar. Seth sighed quietly.

"Let me do that for you. Laz, I'm not a doctor, but you're scaring me. I think you've had a breakdown."

"Then putting me in a strange environment with jaded doctors who don't give a shit and probably think I've been sniffing my own test tubes is not what I need." Lazlo looked at Seth and spoke softly. "I am very fucked up right now. No argument. Don't make it worse by dragging me to a hospital."

Seth finished decorating Lazlo's hotdog with green relish and coarse ground mustard. "Okay. But I'm staying until I know you're better."

"That's fine." Lazlo smiled without humour. "Just don't mess up my stuff."

They sat together on the foam mattress, watching the fire, talking. Lazlo had a bite of his hot dog, but food was not going down easily. Seth gently urged him to finish it, but one more bite was all he could manage. Seth finished it, feeling relieved as Lazlo lay down, willing him to sleep.

"Close your eyes," he said quietly.

Lazlo blinked, his body and spirit exhausted. "Seth?"

"Yeah?"

"If Laird comes by… don't let him in. I think if I see him, I really will die."

Seth gazed down at Lazlo and surprised himself by reaching out to stroke the dark, unruly hair. "Don't worry, Lazlo. He's not getting by me. Not if I have to take a tire iron to him."

Lazlo nodded, then exhaled quietly. Soon he fell into a leaden sleep. Seth stroked his hair for a little while longer, then lay down beside him, gently pulling the sleeping bag over Lazlo. Eventually, he fell asleep himself.

* * *

Laird did not come back. Apparently, he did not even bother to quit his job. He simply vanished, heading back to Florida with Lazlo's money, research, and belongings, leaving Lazlo with a broken heart and a shattered spirit. It was up to Seth and Beth to help Lazlo survive the days that followed. They helped him to apply for an extended leave of absence from work, and Beth bought him some new clothes so he was not with only one outfit to his name. She had to do it without Lazlo present. He would not leave the house.

Seth had not been expecting Lazlo to recover quickly, and he wasn't. He seemed perpetually confused, lost in unending shock and grief. He rarely slept. Instead, he paced the empty confines of his cabin, as if searching endlessly for something he could not find. Laird had been his world, and the emotional blow dealt by Laird's betrayal had all but destroyed him. Seth did what he could to get Lazlo back on his feet, but he wasn't sure Lazlo wanted to get back up, if indeed he was even able.

"You know you can't stay in here forever," Seth said to him one evening as they were roasting a chicken and potatoes in the fireplace.

"I don't see why not," said Lazlo.

"Because you have a life to live."

"Laird was my life."

Seth fought back an urge to scream aloud in frustration. He drew a steadying breath, reminding himself not to make any remarks about what a piece of garbage Laird was. At least, if Laird had died, then Seth could tell Lazlo that Laird would not want him to be alone and unhappy. But Laird was not dead. He was alive and well and living in Florida with another man, taking credit for research Lazlo had done. At least, that was what the postcard he sent had said. Seth had torn it up and burned it before Lazlo saw it.

"Well, how about we go furniture shopping tomorrow?"

Lazlo shook his head. Seth raised an eyebrow.

"Do you really want to be cooking in your fireplace for the rest of your life?"

"No," said Lazlo quietly. "But I don't want to buy furniture either. Because once I buy furniture, you will assume I'm okay, and then you'll leave. I don't want you to leave. I… I'm really not ready to be alone, Seth." He was silent for a little while. "That's really selfish of me, isn't it?"

"Well, kind of," admitted Seth. "It's also perfectly understandable after all you have been through. You know I could sell my house and move in here with you. At least until you're better. There's room out back to work on bikes."

Lazlo shook his head. "Don't sell your house. You love that house."

"I do," said Seth. "But the truth of the matter is I can't stand to be there anymore. Just… too damned many ghosts."

For the first time in weeks, Seth saw a faint spark of light in Lazlo's dark eyes. He turned to look at him and seemed just the smallest bit alive.

"Really? You'd… move in with me?"

Seth smiled. "Sure. Lazlo, I'm your friend. You'd do it for me in a minute, don't try to tell me you wouldn't. But… I'm gonna have to insist on a fridge and an oven. Your well works fine at keeping the beer and stuff cold, but I'm gonna have to draw the line at trying to cook pizza in the fireplace."

"Yeah, it would be nice to make chilli again," said Lazlo quietly.

Seth cast a glance at the potatoes as one began to hiss. "You… uh… did remember to poke holes in those potatoes before you wrapped them in foil and put them in the fireplace, didn't you? So they won't blow up?"

"Of course, I did. I'm sick, I'm not…" Lazlo tried to find the word. "Stupid." He laughed dispiritedly at himself.

"Well, you are still a little addled." Seth's smile broadened slightly. "So… Splog come help Og hunt for appliances?"

The dark eyes looked worried, then Lazlo nodded. "Okay." He glanced down at the mattress upon which they sat, the mattress they had been sharing now for roughly four months. "But… we have a decision to make."

"And what would that be?" asked Seth.

"Two single beds, or one double?"

Seth's brow furrowed. "Laz, it's way too early to be asking questions like that."

"I know. I'm just… wondering, I suppose." A faint smile touched Lazlo's lips. "And… yeah. I was flirting with you in the kitchen that night we made chilli."

Seth laughed. "I knew it! I absolutely knew it."

"Oh, yeah? How?"

"Well, for one thing, none of my other guy friends stand behind me and reach over my shoulder to get something so they can pretend they're not sniffing me."

"You were busy. I didn't want to ask you to move!"

"Uh-huh," said Seth. "Laz, in case no one has told you this and you are not aware of it, you are a short-ass. It would have been far easier for you to wait for me to move rather than flattening yourself out, standing on your toes and pressing the full length of your body against me."

"Easier, but not as fun."

Seth laughed quietly. "It's good to see you smile. It's been a while."

"Four months," said Lazlo quietly. He raised his head and looked out the window at the falling snow. "December now." He sighed.

"Time to get off the floor, maybe." Seth nodded. "Yeah. Maybe it is."

Lazlo used a barbecue fork to turn the chicken. "You… never answered me about the bed," he said, his voice soft.

Seth gazed at his friend for a long time, sorting his feelings. He knew he loved him, but he wasn't certain what sort of love it was. The love of one close friend for another, definitely, but… it wasn't as simple as that. There were underlying emotions he had not had an opportunity to analyze yet. And he could not deny there had been that one moment at Beth's wedding when he had watched Lazlo with his head on his shoulder, softly shining with glitter, where he had felt… something. He didn't know if it was want or desire or just a simple case of the drunk-n-stoopids. But he had to be honest with himself and admit… there could be something with this man, something good, and all he had to do was be brave enough to explore the possibility.

"How about two singles now, with an option to upgrade?" said Seth quietly.

Lazlo glanced at him, surprise in his dark eyes. Clearly, he had expected Seth to simply say 'two singles' and that would be the end of it. After a moment, he nodded.

"Yeah, I think… I think that's good."

They sat in silence for a while, watching the chicken roast in the fireplace. Seth edged closer to Lazlo and tentatively put an arm around his shoulder. Lazlo settled against him comfortably and looked up at him with eyes that had at long last regained some of their brightness. He smiled.

"If I had two specimens of varicella-zoster virus, I'd give you one."

"Gee thanks, Laz, how could I say no to that?" Seth grinned. "Just make sure you keep your Calymmatobacterium granulomatis to yourself."

"Oh, very good, you've been reading!"

"I can, you know."

"Then you know it's not a virus. It's a bacterium."

"I know I don't want it, and that's good enough."

Lazlo smiled, that bright happy Lazlo smile Seth had not seen in four months. Seth felt as if a weight had been raised from his chest at long last. He lowered his head so their brows met, noses touching, gazing at one another.

"So what do you want?" asked Lazlo quietly.

"I don't know," said Seth. "I really don't. I'm going to have to do a lot of thinking before I make any promises, and you need to heal. We've both got a long way to go before we know if we're going to buy that double bed. But… the door's not closed on the idea. And either way it works out, I'm not going anywhere."

"Good," said Lazlo softly.

Seth smiled as Lazlo slowly edged closer, knowing full well what he was about to do. His smile broadened into a grin as he felt a brief, soft meeting of their lips and just the slightest touch of the wet heat of a tongue.

"Always pushing our boundaries, aren't we?"

Lazlo just snorted and settled against Seth's chest, closing his eyes. "Oh, get over yourself," he said quietly.

Seth stroked his hand over Lazlo's hair, and together they sat in peace, watching their dinner slowly roast in the fireplace. At least, that was what they did until the potatoes began to explode.

Chapter 2: Poem - Ocean Waves

He was silver, lying on his side, the moonlight coming
in through the window, turning his flesh to ice, his hair
to mercury. The curves of his body were smooth
and inviting,

Undulant, begging a hand to trace their perfect lines,
down the gentle slope of the ribs, into the dip of his
waist. Back up the rise of his hip, like a ship on the
water,

Cresting the waves in a sea that would soon become a
thrashing storm,

Ending in white spilled across the perfect flat of his
stomach,

Like froth on a beach,

And all became quiet once more.

Chapter 3: October Rain

It was raining. Somehow, that seemed so stereotypical. Like starting a suspense novel beginning with "*It was a dark and stormy night.*" It just seemed like such an obvious way for the weather to be when one was sitting by a new grave in the cemetery.

The Skinny Goth Kid sat on the wet grass, feeling it soak into his black jeans, saturating his long black coat. He shivered and thought that was strange. People were supposed to be anesthetized during times like this, heedless to all else. But he was all too aware of the cold and the wet, the way the rain slid into his face, smearing his black eyeliner and making his clove cigarette go out. He placed the filter between his black-painted lips and relit it with a Zippo lighter, then once more glanced up at the sky, slowly exhaling the fragrant smoke.

"God's a conformist," he grumbled. A fat drop of water hit him in the eye. "And he hates kids," he muttered to himself.

He dried his eye and wished Ryan was there. He would be laughing.

They had met only eighteen months ago: February fourteenth of all days. Ryan was on his way to school. He was seventeen going on eighteen, with blond hair and blue eyes, broad shoulders, wearing a Vancouver Canucks jacket. Not just any Canucks jacket, either – a limited-edition leather jacket, soft golden tan in colour, with the team logo embossed on the back. He looked like a Nice Boy – the kind of Nice

Boy that you see on TV, helping his little sister with her math homework and his dad with the car, but never Mom with the housework because that was Gay.

Skinny Goth Kid was lurking by the dumpster, clove cigarette in one hand, driven there by other Nice Boys, who were Normal and Not Gay. Skinny Goth Kid watched Nice Boy walk by, his green eyes cold and slightly fearful. He waited for Nice Boy to move out of sight, finishing his cigarette. He dropped it in a puddle.

Funny how it been raining that day, too, like foreshadowing or something. God wrote dull and predictable novels.

Goth Kid stepped from behind the dumpster and began heading for the school also, musing how life did not show sympathy for the screw-ups and losers. In fact, it saved the worst garbage for people who already had more than their share. But in four more months, Grade 12 would be over, and he could move on. He could officially leave Childhood Hell far behind.

He stepped forward and crashed chest-first into Nice Boy, who had doubled back to drop something into the garbage. Goth Kid felt his knee twist painfully, and he cried out, collapsing, hands clutching the Canucks jacket, his fingerless black gloves leaving faint traces of dye on that beautiful golden leather. He expected to be dropped to the ground and walked over, but, instead, he was half-carried to an upside-down trashcan and gently seated on it.

Nice Boy asked, "Are you all right?"

Skinny Goth Kid stared, blinking in surprise. He tried to think if anyone had ever asked him that before. He didn't think anyone had.

"My knee pops out," he said quietly. "I broke it when I was a kid."

Nice Boy felt the knee, his expression one of concern. He seemed to know what to look for. Perhaps he played sports. Didn't all Nice Boys play sports? "How did you break it?" he asked.

Goth Kid took out a clove cigarette and lit it. "I don't remember," he lied, not wanting to admit his father had done it with a hammer. "I was pretty young."

Nice Boy examined the knee. "Well… feels like it popped back in. Wanna try standing on it?"

"Nah, I'll give it a minute."

Nice Boy nodded and straightened up, looking a little uncomfortable. The bell rang. He glanced towards the school half a block away, but he didn't depart. He just stood. There was a silence.

"Are those good?" Nice Boy suddenly asked. "The… clove things."

Goth Kid smiled, very faintly. "Well, I like them, but taste is subjective." He offered it to Nice Boy… who just might actually *be* a *nice* boy. He took it and had a drag, then made a face.

"Whoa. Gross." He gave it back. "I'm Ryan, by the way."

So Nice Boy had a name. Wow. Skinny Goth Kid took a drag off his cigarette. "I'm Anaslis."

"Anaslis?"

"It's Irish. My grandmother named me. Her side of the family is Irish, and she wanted to… I dunno… keep with the tradition."

Ryan smiled. "That's cool. I'm named after my mom's great uncle. It's not as cool as Anaslis, but at least she didn't name me after my great aunt."

"I dunno, could be cool. What's her name?"

"Geraldine."

"They could call you Gerry."

"Thanks, I think I'll stick with Ryan. Um… I've never said this to a guy before, but you've got lipstick on your teeth."

"Ah, crap." Anaslis rubbed his finger over his teeth. "Did I get it?"

Ryan laughed. "Yeah, you did."

Anaslis slowly stood up, trying his knee. It seemed okay, but then it went out once more with another agonizing shot of pain.

Ryan caught him before he hit the ground, gently lifting him. "It's cool," he said quietly. "I've got you."

* * *

So that was it. They were friends. They were the most mismatched pair of friends in the school. Ryan was popular and handsome and athletic, with parents who could afford to give him and his sister anything they needed and most of what they wanted. Anaslis was skinny and unpopular and would rather be killed by rabid dogs than do anything that even looked like sports. Despite that, there was an underlying connection between them.

Anaslis was not certain what it could be at first; he had no idea what he could possibly have in common with a kid like Ryan. Anaslis' parents were dirt poor and wouldn't throw him a line if he fell off a ship. His mother was vicious in a malicious, conniving way, and his father was just abusive. Anaslis had boarded up his bedroom door from the inside and chose to get in and out through the ground floor window to avoid them.

"How do you eat?" Ryan asked as the unlikely pair walked to his place after school.

"I found this little bar fridge and cleaned it up, brought it home, plugged it in. I keep stuff in there."

"How do you pay for food? For that matter, where do you get money for clothes and makeup and cigarettes and all the other stuff?"

Anaslis was silent. Finally, he admitted, "I… know a few men who like skinny Goth kids."

Ryan was clearly horrified. He grabbed Anaslis by the forearms and spun him around, staring into his eyes. At first, Anaslis thought Ryan was going to beat him into the ground for being a fag, but as Anaslis looked into those angry blue eyes, he realized that wasn't this issue.

"You're not doing that anymore," said Ryan. "You're with me now."

"With you? What do you mean I'm with you?"

"I mean you're my friend. Not a whore." He slowly released Anaslis, as if suddenly remembering they were on a sidewalk in full view of the neighbours. "You're my friend. If you need money to eat, I'll give it to you."

Anaslis nodded, a little shocked. "Yeah, sure. I'll pay you back."

"No, you won't. And I'll dust you for prints if ever you do."

Anaslis smiled. "That costs extra."

Ryan stared blankly, as if, at first, he didn't understand. Then Nice Boy blushed red to the ears. "Oh, piss off, jerkwad," he muttered.

They kept walking. They reached Ryan's house in only a few minutes. Nice house, nice yard, nice fence… it was all so damn nice. Anaslis wanted to puke. He hated nice. It was like a scab over an infected wound. Pick at the corner just a bit, and the pus began to ooze.

Anaslis walked into the nice house with Ryan. Everything was so clean and neat and new and proper. He distrusted it almost instinctively. Anaslis paused, suddenly feeling wary, wondering if this wasn't all just some sort of trap. He'd met this guy today, and now he was in his house? Ryan was a jock for crying out loud – the natural enemy of the Goth. He'd seen him with the same Barbie and Ken dolls that daily chased him into the area near the dumpsters. Maybe he should just get the hell out of there.

Anaslis jumped when Ryan touched his back.

"You okay? You look a little freaked."

Anaslis stared at him, green eyes lined in heavy black. "Fine," he finally said.

Ryan seemed to guess what he was thinking. "I'm not like those jerks. I play the game, but… I have to."

They kept up the stairs to Ryan's room. It was a nice room. Nice bed, nice furniture, nice sports posters. Anaslis spied a picture of a blond girl in a cheerleading outfit on a nightstand.

"Your girlfriend?" he asked.

"Yeah." Ryan stepped closer, reaching out to take hold of a silver pentagram on a long, delicate chain around Anaslis' neck. "So… you're a Wiccan?"

Anaslis was surprised and impressed. "Yeah. Most people think that means I'm a Satanist."

Ryan smiled. He released the pentagram and picked up a crystal. "And this is for protection, right?"

"Yeah."

Ryan stepped a little closer, his fingers lightly brushing against Anaslis' black T-shirt. He pretended it was accidental at first, but when Anaslis did not protest, he slipped his hand beneath the long black coat and began gently running his hand over his painfully thin ribs, counting each one.

"I don't want you hustling anymore." He lightly rubbed a thumb over a nipple, noticing it was pierced.

"I gotta eat," said Anaslis.

"I'll give you money."

"Won't your parents notice?"

Ryan shook his head, his hand slowly exploring Anaslis' chest and ribs. "Nah. I have a part-time job. I can spend it however I want."

"Won't your girlfriend mind?"

"She might. If I tell her." Ryan looked into Anaslis' eyes. "You're kinda lucky that your parents don't give a shit what you do. I have to be perfect all the time. I have to have the perfect hair, the perfect clothes, the perfect friends, and the perfect girl. I have to get perfect grades, choose the perfect career, and breed perfect grandchildren, *after* I marry the perfect girl. My entire life is planned out in advance, and I have no say about it. My life has to be an extension of my parents' fairy tale."

"It doesn't have to be."

Ryan shook his head. "Some things aren't worth fighting," he whispered. "When your dad is a lawyer and your mom is a shrink, you learn young that it's easier just to do it their way. Because they can do things to you. Put you on meds, lock you up…"

Anaslis was horrified. "They put you on meds and locked you up? For what?"

Ryan smiled without humour. "Being a troubled youth. That's code for wanting to make up my own mind and find out who I wanted to be. Now when I balk at what they have planned, they start sighing and discussing whether I'm relapsing, usually while I'm right there to hear it. That's code for if I don't do what they want, they can put me back there. I'm not going back."

The hand was under Anaslis' T-shirt now, caressing the white skin. The hand found a nipple and toyed with it gently, experimentally, then tugged up the hem of the black T-shirt to expose the skinny, sinewy white body. He lowered his head and closed his lips over the nipple, sucking it.

Anaslis closed his eyes. "And what if they caught you with me?" he asked.

Ryan did not answer right away, simply continuing to lick and tease the nipple. Then he said, "Honestly? I think they'd kill me."

* * *

Anaslis sat in the rain and stared at the headstone, thinking about that first day with Ryan. They had ended up on the bed, fumbling in a clumsy teenaged way, touching, stroking, kissing. Anaslis had experience with sex, but making love was new to him, and it was nice to be there willingly for a change. Ryan was a virgin, at least with other boys, but made up for it with boundless enthusiasm, lying on top of Anaslis, hot and sweaty, thrusting and rubbing with his pants on because Anaslis didn't have a condom and refused to risk passing on any diseases his clients may have given him.

It was nice — *really* nice instead of fake plastic nice. It had been good. It had been the first time Anaslis didn't feel dirty afterwards. Anaslis recalled how they had been lying together in Ryan's bed when there was a knock at the door. Ryan kissed him, and when he spoke, his tone was apologetic.

"My girlfriend. I had invited her over last night. I didn't know I would have found something better to do this afternoon."

"Better let her in," said Anaslis. "I'll creep out a window."

Ryan shook his head. "No, someone will see and report you. Just come downstairs when you're ready." Ryan got out of bed and quickly began dressing. "Bathroom is right there if you need it to… you know… fix your makeup or something."

53

"Speaking of makeup, you have my lipstick all over your face."

Ryan glanced in the mirror. He rubbed at the smudges on his face with his fingertips, then darted out of the room. Anaslis got up and dressed, then freshened his makeup, reapplying the black, anise-flavored lipstick, the white base to make him look pale and unearthly, then the dark eyeliner. He pulled on his fingerless gloves and long black coat, then left the room, heading downstairs.

Ryan was standing with the girl from the photo, as well as three Nice Boys, all of whom at one time or another had taken swings at him. Anaslis tried to pretend he wasn't afraid as the girl turned her head and spied him. She curled her lip, looking him up and down.

"Ew. Who's the vampire?" she sneered. "Did he break in or something?"

The trio of Nice Boys turned to look at him as well. Anaslis stared back at them, doing his best to look cool and disdainful. Ryan interceded before anyone had a chance to say anything further.

"Anaslis is my friend, so lay off him."

The three boys backed off slightly. They never became friendly with Anaslis, but after Ryan said Anaslis was his friend, they at least stopped chasing him. The girl just rolled her eyes.

"Fine. Goth Fag is your friend. Just get him out of here before he gives us bugs or something."

Ryan gave her a cold look and then looked at Anaslis. "Can you stay a while longer?"

Anaslis said, "No, I have to be leaving before I catch Stupid Bitch disease."

The Nice Boys snorted with amusement. Clearly, they weren't crazy about this girl, either. Another point in his favour. Ryan walked Anaslis to the door. Once out of sight of the others, he kissed him and gave him forty dollars.

"Get some food."

Anaslis took the money, looking down at it. "Thanks," he mumbled. "Are you sure about this?"

Ryan nodded. "Yeah. Take it. Will I see you tomorrow?"

Anaslis nodded. "Yeah," he said quietly. He stuffed the two twenty-dollar bills into his pocket. "And… thanks."

"For what?"

"For not… spending the afternoon fooling around with me on your bed and then introducing me to your girlfriend as 'just some guy.'"

Ryan touched his face, saying nothing, uncertain of what he wanted to say. Anaslis kissed him once more, then quietly left.

* * *

They were together every day after that. Sometimes, they went to Anaslis' house and groped and fumbled. Then, after a doctor declared him clean, the groping and fumbling became sex. Good sex at first, then bad sex, finally dropping off to no sex as Ryan began seeing his life for what it would be – a long narrow path to nowhere, with attempts to stray soundly and viciously thwarted. He became depressed, and their precious time together became hours of darkness as Ryan felt the noose close around his neck. Towards the end, they would just lie on Anaslis' dirty sheets, naked, holding each other, saying little.

"There has to be something we can do," said Anaslis quietly one dark October night, his head on Ryan's chest.

Ryan shook his head. "I don't know. I can't see it. They're already talking about when I'm going to marry my girlfriend. I'm not even twenty yet! Jeez, they make me sick! I want to dump her because she's a whining little twit with all the brains of a sack of dog crap, and all I hear is 'Oh, but she's so sweet and cute, and you'd be crazy to dump her, we love her.' Well, why don't they marry her? I don't want to. I'm going to be twenty in March, and I want to live my life."

Anaslis sat up and looked at him, his long black hair falling loose around his shoulders. "We could go away together."

"And do what? Live where? Anaslis, you don't understand, if I announce that I'm moving, they'll take away any money I have and send me to a hospital. Mom will say I'm demonstrating irrational behaviour and delusional thinking. I'll never see you again." He gently drew Anaslis down against his chest, closing his eyes. "I couldn't live with that. I can't lose you."

Anaslis lay with his head on Ryan's chest, feeling a sick lump in his stomach and a crushing ache around his heart. "So what are you going to do with me after you get married? Pass me off as your live-in interior decorator?"

Ryan squeezed his eyes shut, then rolled over, landing on top of Anaslis. He tried desperately for a few minutes to take him, then gave up, lying on Anaslis, holding him tightly. They said nothing more to each other. Then, when dawn came, Ryan dressed and left without a word.

Then, four nights ago, Ryan came to his room in the middle of the night. He undressed and climbed into bed with him, reaching for Anaslis with a hunger he had not shown in weeks. They made love twice, passionately, lying entwined and embracing until the sky began to lighten. Then Ryan kissed him and gave him an envelope.

"Don't open this until just before midnight on October the thirty-first, okay? Promise me."

Anaslis looked at it, his black hair rumpled and spreading around his head like a dark aura. "What is it?"

Ryan kissed him. "Promise me," he whispered.

"Sure. I promise."

Ryan touched his face and gazed at him, as if this was the last time he would ever see him. "I love you. You're all I do love." Then he grabbed his Canucks jacket and was gone.

Anaslis glanced up at the rain, then down at the watch on his skinny white wrist. He couldn't see it, so he took out his Zippo and lit it. Three minutes to midnight. He put the lighter away briefly in order to draw out of his other pocket a black candle and the envelope. He lit the candle, thankful the rain wasn't a torrent. The candle should stay lit just long enough to glance at what he had. He tore open the envelope and dumped the contents out, finding a letter.

My Anaslis,

Five days ago, my parents gave me access to an account – funds for college and university and cash to live on while studying. I checked, and there was just over $250 grand in there. I withdrew the lot without telling them. They told me to spend it wisely because it was the last money they would ever give me. I plan on it.

Anaslis read the letter twice, then glanced up as the beams from car headlights swept across the grass. The vehicle stopped on the wide asphalt path near the grave, and as Anaslis rose to his feet, he heard the passenger side door open. Anaslis picked his battered green duffle bag off the grave and ran to the car, throwing the bag onto the back seat before getting into the front passenger side. He looked at the driver, his mascara running down his cheeks like black tears, his hair lank and wet. He was soaked and shivering and accepted the towel he was offered gratefully.

"So is running away to Toronto and changing your name considered spending wisely?" asked Anaslis.

"Seems like a damn smart idea to me," said Ryan.

Anaslis smiled and leaned forward to let Ryan taste his anise-flavoured black lipstick.

God wrote dull and predictable novels. But once in a while, he added a happy ending.

Chapter 4: Poem -Strange Fish

I don't know how to start.
Nah, that's not it.
I don't know how to stop.
These thoughts just come out of my head like bats escaping a
cave, and no matter how I
try to bar the entrance, they escape.
So maybe it's just gotta be said.

I can't bear to see you, frozen cold and staring,
like the climbers on Everest,
locked forever in time and silence by pain.
I find myself walking down the paths past the silent
memories that line the way,
and pause, thinking "Have I been here before?"
The scent of perfume in the air tells me yes, and I know I
should stop. But I go. Onwards.

Into the dreams, God, the dreams.
Standing in a foreign hotel,
trying to make change for a room with an eleven-dollar bill.
It all makes no sense, the man can't make change,
and I realize that no matter how I try, I'll always be the
outsider.

Sometimes we're in the ocean,
and I watch you play with the sharks you see as angel fish,
the ones always cruising just
outside your perimeter.
They disguise their rancid flesh with bright colours and
sugar-armor, but I'm watching

the candy scales dissolve.
You can't see them. I can't say anything.
I'm under water. I'll drown if I speak.

I swim to the surface.
I wait for you with a towel.

Chapter 5: Forever

"You look a little out of place," said a voice. It was warm and soft, like melted caramel, and had a strange accent that Guthrie couldn't place.

He glanced towards the tall man who had come to stand beside him, offering him a glass of exotic champagne.

"That would be because I feel a little out of place." Guthrie accepted the champagne and sipped it, tasting a faint flavour of strawberry.

"The house takes a little getting used to," said the tall man. He slipped a gentle arm around Guthrie, resting his hand on his back. "Eight floors, more below, more people than we can name living here…"

Guthrie normally did not care for being touched, but there was something about this man that made him want to trust him, made him want to stay beside him, and know safety for the first time in his short tragic life.

"You don't know who is living here? It's your house."

"No, that's not quite true," said the man, tossing back his long auburn hair. "It is my brother's house, but I'm not sure even he knows who lives here. In many ways, the house is its own entity. It decides who to bring here. Oh, how rude, I have not introduced myself. I am Windsor."

"Guthrie."

"Pleased to meet you."

Guthrie allowed himself to be guided across the ballroom-sized living room, gazing around at the grand furnishings worthy of the halls of a deceased robber baron from centuries ago. There seemed to be no electricity, and the only light was from a few candles mounted into ancient holders on the walls, which were covered in silk and velvet wallpaper. The whole place spoke of an eternity of wealth and dignity, and the air within was almost Elven with the weight of the centuries. These people had been here forever. And they would remain forever.

They walked over to an ancient cage-style elevator, stepping into it. Guthrie could not help but notice Windsor seemed vaguely distracted, but not in any unhappy way. Though he looked thirty-two at best, Guthrie could tell he was far, far older, and the years had somehow filtered into his soul and lent him a profound peace. Windsor closed the door with a loud clang and pushed a button. The cage began to slowly rise.

"Are you a vampire?" Guthrie asked and couldn't think why such a thing had left his mouth. He didn't believe in vampires, but… in this house, it did not seem so outlandish an idea they could exist.

"No, but we have them. Three, in fact. Vance, Thaddeus, and one more, Haden. Before you begin wearing iron collars to bed, you will be quite relieved to know that vampires have far more control over their urges than movies like to portray. That is how they manage to stay creatures of myth and legend. We have a werewolf, too. We even have a fallen deity. He has no name, but he likes to call himself Voltaire. Apparently, at one point, he was the god of destiny, but now he dwells here and is a self-proclaimed busybody. I'm actually what you would refer to as a 'space alien' myself. Which is absurd because I never lived in space. I lived on a planet. I and my two brothers and my husband landed here very long ago. My youngest brother found this house, and here we live."

Guthrie smiled. "You don't look like an alien."

A smile touched Windsor's full lips. "Hmm… you say that now. But wait until you get to know me a little better."

"I have so very many questions," said Guthrie as the elevator continued to slowly rise.

"I'm sure you do," said Windsor softly, his intense green eyes warm with compassion and sympathy. "It's hard to end up here. This house can only be found after great personal tragedy and much suffering. I think you know all about pain."

"I do," said Guthrie. He glanced down at himself and realized he was still dressed as a whore – torn leather pants, high-heeled boots, a mesh shirt… all stretched over a skinny body covered in bruises and filth and needle marks. A frown crossed his pretty face as he pushed his shaggy blonde hair out of his face. "I just realized… I'm not high. And… I don't have any cravings."

"You won't. I mean, unless you choose to leave and take up where you left off before the house summoned you. I fear we haven't any control over that."

"Am I dead?"

"No one dies here," said Windsor softly. "This is a place of rest. Not death. It is built upon a liminal, where the curtains between worlds are thin." The elevator stopped, and the door slid open. "Come. This is the fourth floor. Your room is here."

"I have a room?"

"All who come here have a place."

"This house is so beautiful… so elegant! I've never been…"

Guthrie hid behind Windsor's large frame, uttering a startled little cry as suddenly a pair of bats the size of Condors shot by so quickly that the wind of their passing pulled on his hair. They darted down the hallway, then suddenly banked and flew down a wide marble staircase. Guthrie gazed after them, shaking, holding onto Windsor's muscled arm.

"What was that?"

"Vampires," said Windsor dryly. "They like to think they're amusing. Unfortunately, so do some of our other guests. I fear you'll end up dealing with a number of eccentrics."

Guthrie shivered. "I don't like eccentrics."

Windsor placed his hand on his back, comforting him. "No, of course, not," he said sympathetically. "I don't blame you. You have been through a great deal. But once you realize that you are safe and you begin to feel better, you will perhaps be a little better disposed towards them."

"I don't know. Perhaps. I don't trust many people. Except you. And… that's strange because I've known you a few minutes at best."

Windsor smiled. "Well, that's because I am handsome, intelligent, and loveable."

"Uh huh. Modest, too."

"Well, it is a burden to be perfect."

"My heart bleeds for you." Guthrie had another sip of champagne. "This is delicious. I've never had champagne before."

"That is a very rare variety, though, for some reason, we never seem to run out. Other supplies we have to find but never good liquor. And the food never seems to run out, either. However… when you go into the fridge in the kitchen, please be very careful of any unmarked containers. Or even marked ones. We have three geneticists in the house, and… it's just safer if you look before you eat."

"I'll keep that in mind."

He felt his blue eyes grow large as he saw a tall man step out of a room ahead of them in the hall. He was tall, with dark skin and intensely blue eyes that were nearly luminous. He was wearing a dark uniform that Guthrie did not recognize, and he exuded an air of power and authority and of past ages lived. Guthrie took Windsor's arm between his hands and drew close for protection.

"Who is that?"

"That would be my husband. Lovely, isn't he?"

"Why do I feel like I'm about to be demoted, and I'm not even in the military?"

The tall dark man walked over to Windsor, touching his face and kissing him softly. They nuzzled one another and whispered to each other in a strange tongue Guthrie had never heard. The man cast Guthrie a disinterested look, then walked away, Windsor gazing after him.

"Magnificent, isn't he?"

"Damned scary is more like it."

"Yes, well, you don't make General by being cuddly." Windsor smiled dreamily. "Except with your favourite subordinate."

"I'm not ever really sure what that means, but it sounds like too much information."

"Sorry. We came here long ago to save his life. We gave up everything we had to be together. I feared, at first, I would love him less once all the drama was over, but the truth is I love him more now that we do not have to live in fear."

"Sounds like a fascinating story."

"I'll share it with you some day. I think it is, but, then again, I am in it, so I am biased."

Guthrie smiled. "I'd still love to hear it. I wanted to be a write once upon a time. I love fascinating stories."

"Well, that's the lovely thing about being here," said Windsor. "Now you can be. Here we are." They stopped outside an enormous door, elegantly and intricately carved with draperies of flowers gilded in gold. "This is your room."

Guthrie stared at the door, once more clinging onto Windsor's arm, frightened. "What will I find in there?"

"I don't know. It's your room. Nothing goes in there that you don't want."

"And you're sure I'm not dead?"

"Quite sure. You're very much alive."

Guthrie nodded but couldn't seem to make himself let go of Windsor's arm just yet. He felt his knees shake. "I'm so afraid."

"Don't be," said Windsor softly. "There is nothing frightening here." He gently extracted himself from Guthrie's grasp. "Breakfast is at nine if you care to come downstairs to the formal dining hall and meet some of the other inhabitants in the morning. We don't stand much on ceremony here, so do not concern yourself if you're not up to it."

Guthrie nodded, then reached out to open the door, drawing a quiet gasp as he saw the chamber that lay beyond. His blue eyes shone, and he smiled.

"It's so beautiful! It's what I've always wanted my house to look like if I had a house. This is large enough to be a house."

"It's an apartment, really. There are several rooms. All yours."

Guthrie looked up at Windsor. "I don't know how to thank you."

"There's no need to thank me. I did nothing."

The door across the hall opened, and out stepped a rather small man, with fair skin and long black hair. He was dressed in close-fitting jeans and a baggy sweater, and his eyes were a strange shade of reddish-gold.

"Windsor, can I trouble you for just a minute to…? Oh. Hello." He smiled at Guthrie. "Hi. You're new."

"Hello, Haden," said Windsor. "This is Guthrie. You and he are going to be neighbours."

Haden smiled, not bothering to try to hide his impressive fangs. He stepped across the hall to extend his small white hand to Guthrie. "Welcome to the Frank Place."

Guthrie took Haden's hand, eyes fixed on his beautiful face. "Frank Place?"

"Well, that's what we call it. It belongs to Frank, it's his place, ergo…"

"The Frank Place," said Guthrie. "Got it."

Haden smiled, then backed up, suddenly becoming shy as he realized Guthrie was staring. Guthrie himself realized a moment later and also drew back, unable to stop himself from smiling.

"Well, aren't the both of you just precious," said Windsor.

"Bite me, space alien," said Haden. "By the way, do you have a moment to look at my stereo? The speakers died again. I have no idea what's wrong."

"Very well." Both Windsor and Haden looked to Guthrie. "Would you like to join us?" asked Windsor. "We usually end up making a horrid mess, getting drunk, and then finally getting my husband to fix it."

Guthrie glanced at Haden and felt himself blush like a timid virgin… something he had not been in far too long.

"Sure, sounds like fun."

"Great!" Haden reached out and took Guthrie's wrist. "Come on! I'll finally have someone new to bore with my antique porcelain!"

"Oh, I can hardly wait!" said Guthrie dryly.

"Well, what do you want? I died in the seventeen hundreds when there was a deplorable lack of video games."

"Then porcelain will have to do," said Guthrie.

Haden smiled at him, and Guthrie felt his weary heart within him smile a little as well. Together the three went into Haden's room, and there they stayed for hours. It was the first time Guthrie laughed in what seemed like forever.

Chapter 6: Otis Goes to a Wedding

Notes: The author would like to point out this is a *true* story and was filled in on her ferret's antics by the people involved. The white specks on the photos are flecks of latex paint. All pictures are taken at the time of The Great Weasel Escape.

* * *

Otis was a ferret…

…and he lived in Vancouver with his two humans, Alyx and Matthew…

…and his three friends Sharkey, Kipling, and Gryphon, who were all cats.

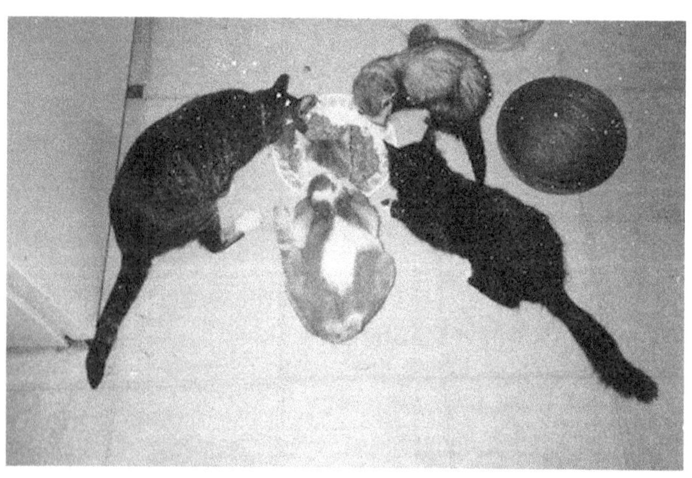

Otis was a young ferret and very adventurous. He loved to go outside on warm sunny days and play in the garden, chasing the bright butterflies that came to rest on the flowers.

Sometimes, Alyx would say, "Let's go for a walk, Otis."

Then she would bring out his blue harness and leash, and off they would go. Sometimes, they just went to the bank or the store. The bank was fun because he could play with the pens on the counter and scatter the papers on the desk and make a big mess. Otis loved to make messes.

But, sometimes, they would just walk and walk and see all the things there were to see. This was the most fun of all because there were always new people to meet. But, for some reason, many of them did not seem to have any idea what Otis was.

A policeman on a great big motorcycle asked if Otis was a mink. Well, that was *pretty* close, Otis thought. He didn't mind that. Then he met two young girls who asked if he was a badger. Well, that was sort of close, too, but Otis didn't think he looked much like a badger. Then a young man with the most amazing green hair asked if he was a seal. No, that was way off base! Otis didn't like water, and he certainly did not like fish. The very worst was when a little boy asked if he was a walrus! A *walrus*? Otis wanted to bite him on the ankles, but Alyx wouldn't let him.

"No," said Alyx, "he is a ferret, and his name is Otis. Walruses are much larger."

Walks were fun, even when people asked if he was a walrus. Otis would have been happy to play outside all day long until it was dark.

However, there were times when Otis did not get to go outside. Sometimes, his humans were too busy to take him out. Then he would sit and stare out the window, watching the butterflies and hoping he would get to go out again soon.

One day, Shane and Norma came over to help his people paint their apartment. Then no one had any time at all! Everywhere were cans of paint, rolls of wallpaper, and boxes of floor tiles. They tore up the carpet and pulled out all the things in the kitchen and made a huge mess.

All the neighbours thought it was great fun to watch, but poor Otis just wanted to go out into the sunshine. Everyone was much too busy to play, except for Gryphon, the orange-spotted kitten. He knew a wonderful game. Why didn't they play Follow the Leader?

Otis played this for a little while, but when Gryphon jumped over the paint pan and Otis tried to follow, there was an awful accident. Otis did not jump very well, and he fell right into the pink paint. After that, little pink footprints followed him around everywhere he went. Otis had almost decided the day was wasted when Gryphon came and whispered something into his ear.

"Did you know," he said, "that the door has been left open? If you are very quick and quiet, you can go out by *yourself* to play!"

Otis went to look, and, sure enough, the door was open. Otis went straight through it and into the yard. He did not stop there, however. There were other places to see. The one place he wanted to see right then was the little white church next door. He had passed it many times, but he had never explored it before. Well, now he would.

He ran straight to the church, but when he arrived, he saw something very odd. There were cars everywhere! Big ones! Blue ones! Little ones and middle ones! But all the cars seemed rather small and plain when he saw the white car. It was so big it seemed to go on forever, and it was white as snow. It glinted and sparkled in the sunlight, and a man in a black uniform stood beside it. He seemed to be waiting for something. Otis stared at the man and the car for a long while, but then he heard music coming from the church, and he went to see what was making it.

He ran up the stairs as best as his short little legs would carry him. He went right up to the doorway and peered into the church. There were many people inside, all seated very quietly. That didn't look like fun, Otis thought. Who wanted to go sit quietly someplace when it was much more fun to run around and scatter things? But then his little bright black eyes caught sight of something.

At the end of the long aisle there stood a woman wearing a beautiful long white gown covered with sparkling sequins and glass beads. On her head was a long train of white lace, and she was holding a large bouquet of white roses. The sequins were so shiny and bright, Otis had to blink his eyes. It was as if someone had taken all the stars out of the sky and put them on the white dress. They were *so* pretty! Maybe that woman would not miss just one. Otis ran down the aisle right up to the woman and jumped up to grab one of the pretty sequins.

The woman did not really have time for little ferrets that day. She was very busy getting married. She was listening to the words of the minister as he spoke his sermon when something pulled very hard at her dress. She looked down, and there was Otis. He was hanging by a sequin from her gown and slowly swinging back and forth. Her mouth hung open as she stared in disbelief.

"There is a *rat* swinging from my dress!" she exclaimed.

The man she was marrying reached down and grabbed Otis, who held onto his sequin very tightly. The man pulled. Otis pulled. There was a great tearing sound. Otis now hung by the scruff of his neck and looked at the crowd of people, his precious sequin in his mouth. For a long time, no one spoke.

"That is no rat!" someone finally said. "That is just a ferret. Pass him to me. He can sit on my lap until the wedding is over."

The man passed Otis to Aunt Mary, who had asked for him, and she put him on her lap. Otis curled up quietly, deciding just to watch now that he had his sequin. But, because he was only very young, he fell asleep and slept through the rest of the wedding.

The next thing he knew, he was being carried out of the church. As he opened his eyes, he saw that he was going with the bride and groom to the big white car. The man in a uniform held the door open for them, and they, along with Otis and Aunt Mary, all got inside. Then they drove off, a long line of cars following them, all honking their horns.

Otis had never been in a car before, and he looked out the window the whole time they were driving. Finally, they came to a large house that had been decorated for the party to follow the wedding. There were paper streamers and silver bells hung in the doorways. A man was taking pictures of all the people. Otis thought this was just wonderful. There were so many people, and they all wanted to pet him and hold him. They gave him many treats from a huge table full of food, and he was allowed to get into all the mischief he liked, putting his head in shoes, climbing up dresses, running across furniture. No one seemed to mind!

The bride, whose name was Kathy, said "Why don't we take some pictures with the little ferret in them to remind us of him? I suppose we will have to find out who owns him, but we can have some pictures!"

More fun! Otis had never had his picture taken. Now he had more pictures taken than he ever wanted. There he was with Kathy and her new husband, her mom and dad, all her aunties and uncles, and her grandpa. Then they took a picture of him in grandpa's boot. Finally, they took one last picture of him on the table, eating cake. It was all very wonderful, but by now Otis did not feel so well. Then he had a drink of some bubbly stuff in a fancy glass, and that did not help at all.

By the time everyone was ready to go home, Otis was asleep in grandpa's boot, dreaming about chasing the butterflies in his own backyard. Otis went home that night with Aunt Mary. He slept on the car seat next to her the whole way home. He was a tired little ferret. It had been a long day.

Meanwhile, back at home, everyone had realized that Otis was not home, and everyone was looking and calling. But no matter what they did, they could not find him. He was not under the neighbour's bush, and he was not under the bed or in the laundry pile. He was not in the bathroom cupboards or the storage closet. He simply wasn't *anywhere*.

Alyx and Matthew were both very worried about him. They thought perhaps he had been stolen or was lost. They sat up most of the night, hoping he would come back. But when morning came and he was still not home, Alyx phoned the newspapers. She told them she had lost her ferret, and if anyone saw him, could they please phone her.

Now it just so happened that Aunt Mary had phoned the same newspaper just a few minutes before. This made the man at the newspaper think that maybe, just maybe, they were talking about the same ferret. He asked Alyx if she lived near the white church on Twelfth Avenue, and when Alyx said yes, he told her about Aunt Mary's call and gave her the phone number. Alyx called Aunt Mary, who said yes, she had a ferret, and it sounded a lot like the one she had lost.

Alyx asked her friend Dan to drive her over to Aunt Mary's house. All the way there, she was nervous. Oh, it had to be Otis, it just *had* to be! She was very worried it might not be. Finally, they reached the house, and Alyx ran up the steps to knock on the door. Aunt Mary answered and led Alyx into the living room where Otis was.

"He's sleeping right now," she said, "but you can still look and see if he belongs to you."

Alyx walked into the living room and saw Otis. There he was, flat on his back, all four little black feet in the air. All around him on the couch were cookies, grapes, raisins, and crackers. Otis did not even notice Alyx had come for him. He was much too full and sleepy.

"Yes," said Alyx, "That's my Otis, and after all the worrying I did, I find him here, too full to care that he is going home."

Alyx thanks Aunt Mary for taking such good care of Otis and got back in the car, Otis on her lap. Otis was too full, and he had a stomachache from everything he had eaten at the wedding party. He was very quiet the whole way home. Then, once he got there, all he did was crawl onto the sofa and go back to sleep. A little while later, Gryphon came to take a nap with him, and Matthew put a blanket over both of them. Everyone was glad to see him back home.

"So just where did you go?" asked Gryphon that evening when Otis finally felt well enough to talk.

"I went to a wedding," said Otis. "And I ate so much that I didn't feel well, and my stomach hurt."

"So," said Gryphon, "I guess there won't be anymore adventures for you!"

"Well," said Otis thoughtfully, "no more weddings, perhaps, but there is that house across the street…"

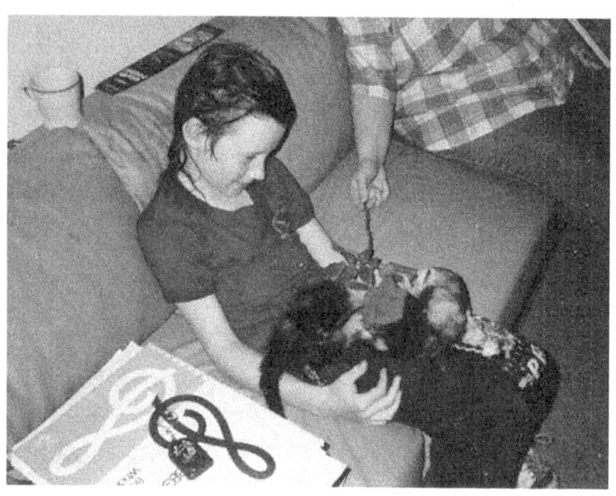

Chapter 7: Road Trip

They drove along in silence, no sound save for the truck's wipers dutifully scraping water off the windshield and the quiet sound of tires on the road. It was late, and it was dark, and there were no lights at all on the rural road, making the long dark drive eerie. Occasionally, animal eyes gleamed out of the long grass at the side of the road, and once a coyote darted out in front of them, avoiding the truck by a hair's breadth. It was an unnerving event early into the drive, and there were five hours to go. Inside the cab of the old pickup truck, the two friends sat in leaden silence.

Daniel could not for the life of him remember what had made him think this would be a great chance to tell Jack that he was in love with him.

True, it did prevent the older man from walking away from him, which had been an issue. Jack was not a man who liked discussing feelings. However, Daniel had failed to recall Jack's innate magical ability. His anger could lower the temperature in any given area and worked twice as well in a small, contained space. Like, say, for instance, the inside of a truck cab.

Emotionally, it was about forty degrees below absolute freezing, and Daniel was as far on the other side of the cab as he could get, lest one of Jack's fists suddenly launch of its own volition and crack him in the nose. It had happened once before, when Jack found out Daniel was the one who left the paddock gate open and Jack's favorite horse had made it three miles down the road to Randy Croft's house and broke into a barrel of apple cider that he had fermenting in his shed.

Getting the plastered Percheron loaded and home had not been fun. On the drive back, Jack's fist had somehow jabbed out suddenly on its own and cracked him on the nose. Daniel was not taking chances on it happening again. Safely out of fist range, Daniel tried once more to express his feelings.

"Jack…"

Jack kept his eyes on the road but showed him his fist. Daniel was not stupid, but, as his mother had pointed out often enough, he never did know when to quit.

"Look, I don't see…"

"Get glasses."

"You are going to let me talk about this."

"No, I ain't." Jack kept his eyes on the flat, straight Alberta road.

"I love you."

"That's nice."

Daniel stared at the older man. He was handsome, lean, and strong, like something out of a movie: just a hair past his prime but still virile and, oh, so damned beautiful. Daniel wanted him so badly, it made his heart break. He had wanted him since he came to work five years ago.

For five whole years, Daniel had, cautiously, let him know that he would like to be a little more than friends, but Jack never seemed to pick up what Daniel was laying down. At first, he thought Jack knew and was simply not interested, but, as time passed, Daniel realized that, no, Jack just couldn't catch a hint unless you mashed it into his face. So he made the hints bigger. Once, he even flat out asked Jack if he would like to go to bed. He still recalled the way Jack stared at him, surprise in his brown eyes.

"Ain't tired," he'd said.

Daniel had fought a temptation to get down on his hands and knees and bash his head on the floor. Instead, he'd just said, "All right," and left.

So, finally, Daniel decided that on the long drive back home from a trip into Edmonton, he would tell Jack he loved him. Daniel was not surprised in the least to find out that, after five years of hints, innuendo, and the occasional touch, the admission was news to Jack.

"Well, what's wrong with me loving you?"

"I'm a married man. And you're just a man."

"Jack, Lauren left you a year ago."

The brown eyes stayed on the straight, narrow rural road. "She might come back."

"Yeah, and monkeys might fly out my ass."

"That, too."

Daniel groaned. "You really are a pain in the ass, you know that. Look, I love you. What's wrong with me loving you?"

"I told you. I'm a man. So are you."

Daniel sighed and sank back into his seat. Then he raised an eyebrow and gave Jack a sidelong look. He knew how to get the old crank to talk. He blinked a few times hard to make his eyes shine wetly and then sniffed. Right on cue, Jack hit the brakes and pulled off the road.

"Aw, don't do that, Christ, don't do that!"

Bingo, thought Daniel. Defensively, tearfully, he said, "I ain't doing nothing! Just drive!"

"I can't drive if you're crying!"

"I ain't crying!"

"You're crying, and I can't deal with it!" Jack turned in his seat to face the younger man. "And what in the hell are you in love with me for?"

"How should I know? What were you in love with Lauren for?"

That was a good question, one that made Jack sit back in surprise. He had loved her, probably still did, and why not? She had been kind, pretty, funny, intelligent. There was a lot to love. But she had come out to look after Jack's son in the last few years of his short life, and if she loved anyone, it was Nathan. She was his caretaker until the end of his days and likely the reason she married Jack was to keep alive some connection to the young man. The marriage lasted a year. Then she moved back to the city, leaving Jack alone with memories of his deceased wife and son, and of the young woman who was kind and compassionate but did not love him back. It was a lot for him to think about.

Quietly, he turned to face the steering wheel once more. He carefully put the truck in drive and started forward. Daniel said nothing, and they drove on in silence. At least the emotional temperature in the cab had gone from icy to neutral.

They reached a small roadside café and stopped to stretch their legs and grab a bite to eat. Jack was still quiet, and Daniel let him be with his thoughts. Jack was not what one might call a sensitive new age guy. He was a fairly basic individual, not stupid or foolish but not terribly introspective. Daniel had given him a lot to chew over, and as the young man watched him sip his coffee, he could tell the wheels were turning. He desperately wanted to ask what Jack was thinking, but a roadside diner in rural Alberta was not the place to continue their discussion.

As Jack had once observed, "It ain't 2006 everywhere in the world, y'know."

Of course, Jack had been referring to computers, not gay relationships. But he had a point.

They ate their dinner. It was a good meal, simple and filling, and Jack had three pieces of apple pie afterwards. How he could eat like that and stay as rangy as he was, Daniel had no idea. If he ate the way Jack did, he would be a thousand pounds inside of a year. But Jack always ate when he was confused.

Jack ate a lot.

They paid for their dinner and left the café, heading for the pickup truck. Jack paused to light a cigarette.

Daniel grinned. "C'mon, Marlborough Man. Hey, I heard he was gay."

"Who?"

"The Marlborough Man."

Jack snorted. "I heard he cacked off from lung cancer."

"That, too."

Jack hrumphed and got into the truck. Daniel hopped into the passenger's side, and they were off once more. Three more hours to go, and the emotional temperature was up from neutral to pleasant. Jack turned on the cassette player, and they drove along through the rain, listening to The Mamas and The Papas. Daniel stared out the window at the rain, listening to the music. For over half an hour, there was a pleasant silence between the two men. Then Jack cleared his throat.

"So… um… how long…" He cleared his throat again. "How long have you felt this way?"

"Since I first saw you," said Daniel quietly.

Jack raised an eyebrow. "That long? Really?" He looked puzzled, as if thinking.

Daniel grinned, hearing the wheels in Jack's mind grind and screech and slooooooowly start to turn. Suddenly, Jack's brown eyes went large.

"You asked me to go to bed with you!"

"Yeah, I did," admitted Daniel. "And you looked right at me with those big brown eyes and uttered the immortal phrase, 'Ain't tired.' Never wanted to hit myself over the head so bad in my life."

"You should have hit me over the head."

Daniel gave him a puzzled look. "Why?"

"Because it was a stupid thing to say!"

"You say stupid shit all the time. If I hit you every time you said something stupid, I'd be up for murder."

Jack's fist flew out and connected with Daniel's shoulder. "Don't be a smart ass."

"Ow! Look, you hit me one more time, you old fart, and I'll take you out back and beat you to death with your own stupidity."

"Ain't old."

Daniel rubbed his shoulder. "No, but you're mean."

Jack thought about that. "Sorry." He glanced at Daniel. "You okay?"

"Yeah, I'm fine, just watch the road."

Jack did, but Daniel could tell the wheels were still turning in his mind. Slowly. Painfully. Grinding against one another with a scream of metal and leaving a cloud of rust.

Why in hell did he love this man?

Two hours to go, and Jack spoke again. "Don't seem fair."

Daniel looked at him. "What doesn't?"

"That you feel this way, and I just ignored you."

"You didn't ignore me. You didn't know."

"I should have, though. I should have known."

Daniel turned in his seat to look at him, studying his face in the faint light of the cab. It was a strong, handsome face, almost aristocratic. A face better suited to a warrior of old than a slightly broken-down rancher. Daniel felt a pain in his heart. Jack deserved better, so much better than what he had.

"I wish you had," he whispered.

Jack swallowed. "Maybe… maybe I don't know what I want. Certainly never put a lot of thought into it."

Daniel dared to move a bit closer. "You can think about it now."

"Not so sure it's a good idea. It ain't 2006 everywhere in the world, y'know."

Daniel grinned, raising an eyebrow in surprise. "Why, Jack Powers, does that mean I have a chance here?"

"Don't mean nothing!" he snapped, but Daniel knew if he was really upset by the remark, he would have hit him. The road curved slightly, and Jack smoothly followed it. "Light me a cig, Danny."

Daniel lit them each a cigarette and passed one to Jack. Jack took it and placed it between his lips. Things were silent again.

One hour from home, Jack said softly, as if in response to a question, "Yeah, I think I could."

Daniel felt a strange rush through his body, and his heart lurched in his chest. Adrenaline coursed through him almost violently, and he felt his jeans tighten slightly.

"You could?" he asked hoarsely, half-afraid Jack was talking about getting a new riding mower or some such thing. That would be typical Jack to forget everything that had happened in the last few hours.

Jack nodded. "Yeah, I think I could." He looked at the younger man, brown eyes soft. "I'm not getting any younger, Danny. My wife is dead, my son is dead, my second wife has left me. The ranch is not doing well, and let's face it, the only reason it's surviving at all is because of you. You and your… love… for an absolute fool."

"I don't love a fool," said Daniel. "I love you."

Jack shook his head. "If I had any sense, I'd pack things in and move instead of letting you spend money buying me new stock."

"I wanted to do it. It's not all altruism, you know. If it saves your ranch, then it saves my job, and now that I'm a partner, if you do well, I do well." He swallowed, watching the face of the man beside him, watching the worry in his eyes. "I did it because I care about you."

Jack shook his head but said nothing further. Daniel watched his face in the light of the cab. Jack was not the brightest bulb on the Christmas tree, but he was a good person. He deserved more than what he had in life. His first wife Nancy had been a good person, too. Daniel had known her in the final year of her life. She had been a quiet, uneducated woman, but intelligent and wise. Daniel liked her and her son Nathan. They had all been horrified by her sudden and violent death, Jack especially. He'd walked around in a daze for the first year after she had been kicked to death by his best stallion. The loss had nearly killed him, and the news two months later that his son was terminally ill had drained away more of his will to live. In his typical quiet way, Jack did what needed to be done to care for him, including hiring an in-home caregiver when Nathan came home from the hospital to die.

A year after Nathan's death, 'Mad Cow' claimed his stock, and Jack had to lay off his employees. Six months after that, Lauren left him to return to the city. What had once been a home and ranch full of life and people and animals was now a sad and silent little shack out in the middle of nowhere.

Daniel stayed on as a renter, paying a small sum to live in the little house behind Jack's that had once been the home of the ranch foreman. He had some money saved, money he had been planning to use to start a small farm where he could breed and raise horses, but when Jack began talking about giving up and selling his ranch, Daniel instead used the money to buy Jack some good beef cattle and to get himself a Friesian stallion.

The horse had not been part of the plan, but… well… Daniel really wanted it.

They drove the rest of the way back to the little house that Jack called home in silence. He parked the truck, and they got out, walking quietly side by side up to the porch. Normally, Daniel would go to his own little place behind the house, but this time, he knew he did not have to. Jack unlocked the door, and they walked into the darkened kitchen. The door closed, and the two stood facing each other in the near-perfect darkness.

For a long moment, neither moved. Then Jack stepped closer, reaching for the younger man, gently pulling him close. Daniel sighed and put his arms around him, resting his head on his shoulder. He closed his eyes and breathed a single word.

"Finally."

He felt Jack's hands come to cautiously rest on his back, then slowly, uncertainly, explore him, touching him.

"Haven't a clue what to do with you," he admitted sheepishly.

Daniel smiled. "I will show you," he said softly. He raised his head and looked into Jack's eyes. "Or maybe you could just kiss me and see where it goes from there."

"Just so you know, I'm lousy in bed."

"Who told you that?"

"Two wives, several girlfriends, and a hooker."

Daniel winced. "Well, we'll work something out, I'm sure."

"Yeah," said Jack quietly. "We will."

They held each other, gazing into each other's eyes. Finally, Jack inclined his head forward, and at last they were kissing. Daniel felt his body go weak, and it was all he could do to stay on his feet. He had wanted this so badly, so long, and never thought he would ever have it. He wondered what Jack was thinking and if, in the morning, he would regret what they had done. Daniel returned the kiss passionately, parting his lips, letting Jack take the upper hand. He was more than happy to submit if it was what Jack wanted.

They kissed, holding each other tightly, touching one another. Daniel let Jack's hands wander on their own, allowing the older man to guide the pace of their first time together. He finally had Jack in his arms after all this time; he did not want to scare him off.

Jack broke off the kiss and said softly, "Too old for messing around on the floor. Let's go to my room."

Daniel nodded, and the two walked towards the bedroom, arms around each other. They entered the small, neat room, and Jack closed the door behind them. Daniel removed his boots and lay down on the bed, feeling the bed creak as Jack came to lie beside him. He drew Jack into his arms and closed his eyes, breathing out a sigh of pleasure as he felt Jack kiss his neck. Funny how Jack could set him on fire like this, how just feeling his hands reach for the buttons on his shirt was more erotic than anything he could think of. He relaxed, closing his eyes, offering himself up like a sacrifice, letting the one he loved caress and slowly explore his young, strong body. He hoped this moment never ended.

An hour later, Daniel was just about out of patience.

He was currently on his stomach, naked, while Jack tried to figure out how to mount him. So much for letting Jack slowly figure this out on his own; the man couldn't take direction if his life depended on it. His sexual catch phrase seemed to be "Give me a minute, I'll get it."

Jack shoved into him, and Daniel raised his head.

"Jack!"

"What? That's where it goes, isn't it?"

"Look, I'm not a mare, and you're not trying to breed me. We're supposed to be making love."

"I thought we were!"

"Off!"

Jack moved off of him, and Daniel sat up to face him.

"Jack, I love you, and I think you are easily the most attractive man I have ever seen. But I gotta say, the two wives, several girlfriends, and the hooker were right."

Jack looked hurt but let Daniel push him gently down to the bed.

"You've never been with a man before, have you?"

Jack shook his head. Daniel kissed him.

"So let me show you, okay?" He grinned. "If you're good, I'll take you out Saturday to see *Brokeback Mountain*."

"Not interested. Why should I watch a film about two guys watching someone else's stock when mine's all dead?"

Daniel raised an eyebrow. "Well, that's one way of looking at it, yes. But it's about two cowboys in love."

"You mean sheepboys. And unless those sheep all die horribly, I ain't going."

Daniel sighed. "In that case, we'll just stay home and watch *Blazing Saddles*."

"Good, I like that one." He stroked his hand down Daniel's thigh and said quietly, "Okay. So show me."

Daniel lowered his head and kissed him. "First off, it's okay to touch me."

"I did touch you."

Daniel lay down beside him and took one of Jack's hands. "Well, you started off good, but then you shied away." He drew Jack close and kissed him, then placed the hand on his hip. "Touch me. Like this. Slowly."

Jack did, stroking his hand over Daniel's slim body, feeling the soft skin over the toned, lean muscle, allowing Daniel to guide where his hand went. He finally drew it down to his penis and made a quiet sigh of pleasure as Jack's hand softly closed around it. He released Jack's hand and relaxed, feeling him touch and caress him. Jack leaned over to kiss him, and Daniel slid his arms around his neck, holding him close.

He felt Jack gently push him, and he complied, moving onto his back, letting the older man get on top of him.

"Easy," he whispered. "I'll show you."

"Give me a minute, I'll get it."

"No way. Jack!"

"What?"

"Not so rough! Geez!"

Jack kissed him. "Sorry."

Daniel rolled his eyes. Why the hell did he love this man? He closed his eyes. "If you finish in forty seconds, fall off, and go to sleep, I'll smother you with a pillow, I swear."

"I'll have you know I can go at least forty-five."

Daniel laughed and drew his legs up. He closed his eyes and wrapped his arms around Jack's shoulders, feeling him move inside of him.

"I love you," he said quietly, simply.

Jack didn't say it back, but that was fine. Daniel knew he was not good with voicing his emotions. He didn't have to be. There was so much more to him than his ability to communicate or how much money he made…

Jack cried out, pushing in hard, spilling semen deep into Daniel's young body. He groaned in pleasure, then rolled off of him, panting.

… or how good he was in bed.

"Fantastic," Jack said emphatically.

Daniel looked at him. "Oh, you *have* to be kidding."

"What?"

Daniel moved over top of him, gently pinning him down, grinning. "Okay, cowboy, you had your chance. Now it's my turn. And I've got all night to show you how to do it right."

Jack stared up into Daniel's sea green eyes. "So, I take it that it wasn't good for you."

Daniel kissed his nose. "No. It wasn't." He reached out for his half-used tube of lubricant.

"Well, give me time, I'll get it."

Daniel grinned evilly as he squeezed some of the slick substance into his hand. "You're darn right you will, cowboy."

Jack looked distinctly worried. "Well, I hope you're not as bad as I am."

Daniel laughed. "Jack, I don't know why I love you, but I do."

Jack laughed quietly and shook his head. "I don't know why you do either." He closed his eyes and relaxed, letting Daniel take control. "But I'm glad you do."

Outside the little house, the storm continued on, beating down on the roof and the red truck and the barns that would soon be full of cattle and horses again. All seemed peaceful, awaiting anxiously the arrival of the new day and the new animals.

Suddenly, Jack's voice echoed across the yard.

"Hey!"

"And now you know why I keep telling you not to be so rough."

"I knew partners were a pain in the ass, but…"

"Jack?"

"Yeah?"

"Shut up and kiss me."

Chapter 8: Poem – Walking on the Moon

Come for a walk on the Moon, they said.
It will be a great deal of fun.
For the life of me I cannot see, how anything here
could be a walk or a run.

A bounce, perhaps, or a boink or a bump.
Or a roll, like a ball on a beach.
To bonk down a hill is too much of a thrill.
I'm sure they can hear me screech.

Boom now as I hit a crater That flings me up into the
stars.
It takes too long to fall, I don't like this at all, this trail
truly needs safety bars.

Now I'm off to the sea, which one shall it be? Mare
Crisium, Nectaris or
Vaporum?
Truly awful I say, let's all go away
Since I can't find a rhyme for Vaporum.

So that was my walk in the deep lunar chalk, I must
say I'm glad to be done. I
want to go home, never more shall I roam to a place
where I can fall up to the
sun.

Chapter 9: Second Christmas

"I hate Khalzi. I mean I really, *really* hate them. Not the way kids hate green beans, or the way my sister hates anything that doesn't have a Gucci label. I mean flat-out-despise-would-kill-if-I-got-a chance hate. And not just because my ex-boyfriend is shacked up with one. But because they bite. And not just bite, but de-glove. That's a medical term I learned. Man, I hate Khalzi, just kill them all and turn them into furry freaking hats…"

The drunken blind man gestured towards the bartender for another drink. Being a Khalzi himself, the tall, beautiful creature selected a dirty mug and filled it from assorted leftover pitchers on the bar before bringing it to him. The drunk took the mug with his left hand, his right tucked under his jacket. He was no more than forty, but years of hard living had aged him, so he appeared to be in his mid-fifties at least, and not a well-preserved mid-fifties at that. The two men seated with him saw, of course, what the Khalzi did but said nothing. Their own beer came icy cold from the taps and in clean mugs. The drunk kept talking.

"I met Liam three years ago in a dump called The Asteroid Bar and Grill. He was a fighter pilot, training aboard Sferkkaan planet hoppers as part of some sort of goodwill exchange between Earth and Sferkkaa. I was waiting tables. Why he looked twice at me, I will never know. Sferkkaans are beautiful, beautiful people, and he was sitting with five guys that I would have gladly reached up my own ass and hauled my heart out to show them just for the privilege of having them spit on me. Gorgeous, eerie, ethereal beauties that just should not exist. And Liam just kept looking at me."

The drunk took a long pull at his beer, oblivious to the old cigarette butt floating in it.

"And I just kept looking at the Sferkkaans. I mean, okay, so I messed around on him a few times, like what's the big deal? Every guy does it. And he totally overreacted when I gave the medal that he won rescuing fifteen civilians and flying them to safety in the middle of the night during a thunderstorm in a plane damaged by anti-aircraft fire to that luscious twenty-year-old whose name I can't remember. But, man, what an ass…. So, anyway, he moved out. Just packed his stuff and vanished one night while I was out clubbing. I mean, you'd think he would at least let me know. Just because I hadn't been home in four days is no excuse…"

One of the two men seated with the drunk, a Sferkkaan himself, raised an eyebrow. "Such ingratitude."

The drunk ignored him. "And, of course, after he was gone, I realized too late how much I did love him and what a bastard I was. Far too little, far too late. I had the love of the most handsome, brave, funny, intelligent guy on the planet, and I blew it. So like any loser, I set out to win him back. I sent flowers, I sent poems, I sent singing telegrams, I even stole his medal back for him. I followed him everywhere. I even left notes on his plane. Okay, so I stalked him. Sue me. I followed him around for five months, begging and pleading on my hands and knees, and then, one night, I see him with a freaking Khalzi. I mean a *Khalzi*! That's two steps from doing it with your dog. Nothing like a seven-foot marsupial to get the neighbours talking. A Khalzi. You could have knocked me over with a feather."

The Khalzi bartender flattened his ears. The Sferkkaan had a feeling the next beer the drunk ordered would be flavored with Khalzi saliva. The drunk rambled on.

"They were in the park, which, of course, is where you take an animal. Khalza was found about ninety-five years ago, and its inhabitants were found, I suppose, around the same time. No one has ever been able to establish if the inhabitants of Khalza ever came to earth, but if you want to know what they look like, then open a book on Egyptian archaeology and find a picture of Anubis. We're talking seven feet of hot man flesh covered in short black fur with the head of a jackal, a mane, and one thing Anubis did not have – a tail. A long soft fox-like tail. Another thing these critters have that Anubis did not is a pouch. Remember the pouch. It's important."

The bartender's lip curled slightly, then he stalked off to clean tables in preparation of closing.

"Actually," belched the drunk, "only the *males* have a pouch. And only the males form villages. The females are sort of free-roaming forces of nature. They roam wild, alone or with other females, and only pay attention to the males when they want a little hot fuzzy love. Then she's off again. If she's pregnant, then after eight weeks, she finds a village, passes something that's more fetus than baby, and hands it off to the nearest male, who sticks it in his pouch while she goes off to do the whole thing over again. It doesn't even have to be his baby… puppy… whatever. Nope. He just shoves the little bastard into his belly pouch and bounces off with the other kangaroos. He doesn't even have to ever had sex with a female. All he has to do is pick up that nauseating pink squirming slug and stick it in his pouch. Nauseating. And there's my Liam with a Khalzi. It was more than I could stomach. I went walking up to him and dog-boy. He was wearing a black leather flight jacket. He was another pilot! Didn't know they could teach dogs to fly a jet."

The bartender reached his limit. He threw down the cloth and called out to the three at the table, "Time, gentlemen, if you please."

"We'll leave when we're done," roared the drunk, slurring his words. He continued with his story. His two listeners worked on getting their beer down before they left.

"Khalzi. Bloody Khalzi. He dumped me for a dog. Me! Can you believe it? Well, okay, he never was bright, but you'd think he would have at least had brains enough to keep with his own kind. Well, we argued for a bit, and I accused him of making puppies with the thing. I guess I might have had a beer or two in me at the time. Anyway, I reached out to grab the pouch and look inside. Nothing hard, I just wanted to look. Bad move. You don't touch a Khalzi's pouch. That's like coming up to strange woman and sticking your finger up her…"

"Time, gentlemen," repeated the bartender.

The drunk waved him off. "So I grab the pouch, and he sinks his teeth into my arm and degloves it. Degloves. You know what that is? It's when something yanks the flesh off in one whole piece, as if pulling off a glove."

The drunk pulled forth what was left of his right arm, which was gone from about the mid forearm down, and with his left mimed yanking off a glove. "Stripped the meat right off. Then the piece of crap goes for my face. Totally unprovoked. Sank his teeth right into my eyeballs. They popped like…"

"Time!" shouted the bartender, shoving a chair hard against the table for emphasis.

The Sferkkaan and his companion rose to their feet. The drunk sat, huddled over his beer, and did not seem to notice the departure of his companions. The two walked out of the little pub and into the warm, starless darkness of a Sferkkaan night. They made their way down the quiet street, saying nothing as they headed to the little hotel where they were currently residing.

The Sferkkaan pulled out a pack of cigarettes and offered one to his companion, a man from Earth currently living on Sferkkaa. Liam took the offered cigarette and sighed heavily, placing it between his lips and lighting it, the faint lines of colour on his uniform blazing briefly in the glow of his lighter.

"Are you sorry you came?" asked the Sferkkaan.

Liam shook his head. "No, Fearyn, I'm not. I needed to hear it. I needed to prove to myself once and for all that I did the right thing walking out on him."

Fearyn raised one eyebrow. "You were not thinking of going back to him, were you?"

"No! Of course, not. But… I did feel badly about the way I ended it. I just… needed to settle some things in my mind. Wow, he looks like crap. Hard to believe it was only eighteen months ago."

"Shar certainly worked him over."

Liam's green eyes grew cold. "Shar was provoked. Rick didn't just try to look in his pouch, which you do *not* do with a Khalzi, but he stuck his whole fist in it, just shoved it right in. Shar screamed. The bastard really hurt him. I'm not surprised Shar bit him. I *am* surprised Shar didn't do more damage than he did."

Liam took a long drag off his cigarette, plainly angry, his voice rising. "I mean, you do not treat a Khalzi that way. He tore up delicate capillaries and membranes. Hell, Shar was in the hospital for two days. And Rick actually has the nerve to sit there, sucking back booze and making himself out to be the victim. I don't get it. I just do not get it."

A voice called something in Sferkkaan from the window of an apartment. Liam responded in the same tongue, turning slightly red. That was one of the reasons Liam liked Sferkkaa so much: polite people. No "Shut the fuck up you asshole!" Instead, he heard, "Need I remind you both of the hour?" Sferkkaan culture in many ways was not so different from that of Earth. But in other ways, it truly was another world. Liam felt Fearyn put an arm around him.

"Rick is a self-absorbed bastard who would not know a good thing if it bit him on the leg," he said.

"Ignore him. Put him out of your mind. He is not worth your anger."

"It's not just Rick," said Liam, mindful now of how loudly he spoke. "It's that attitude. It's *that* attitude in *this* century. You heard what he said about Shar. 'May as well be doing it with the dog, the park's where you take an animal, you should stick with your own kind.' And what was it he called the baby when the female hands it off to the male? Oh, yeah. A nauseating pink squirming slug. Human beings were supposed to be past that sort of crap by now."

"It will happen as long as humans and humanoids exist," said Fearyn. "There will always be those afraid of what is different, of what they do not understand."

"Sferkkaans don't act like that."

Fearyn laughed. "Oh, I beg to differ, my friend. Walk up to any Sferkkaa and utter the word 'Kyphisian.' You will hear a most comprehensive list of racial slurs."

"That's not the same. Kyphisia overran your planet and tried to eradicate your people."

"True. But the point remains the same. No race is without hate and prejudice. Sometimes, it is understandable. Usually, it is not."

Liam sighed. "You're right, of course." He took another drag off his cigarette. Sferkkaans all smoked like Victorian factory stacks. It was hard to live on their planet without picking up the habit. At least they grew excellent tobacco.

Liam glanced at his friend. Fearyn was truly beautiful. Most Sferkkaans were, but Fearyn was a rare sort of beauty, the offspring of a Sferkkaan mother and a Kyphisian father. He was ice-white all over, flesh and hair, with the most intensely blue eyes Liam had ever seen, eyes like a jungle cat on a branch looking down at the unwary. Liam had tried for the longest time to get into his pants, but Fearyn had been with his lover Faunnis for fifteen years. He was not about to throw that away on a fling with some human.

Over time, Liam and Fearyn had become close friends. Liam would still not kick Fearyn out of his bed for eating crackers, but he enjoyed his company too much to lose his friendship over wanton lust.

"It still just bothers me," mumbled Liam. "When I told my mother I was gay, she… wasn't exactly happy about it. In fact, she begged me to get help. Wept for days, followed me around, demanding I tell her who did this to me, like it was a disease someone gave me. I finally shut her up with a book I found about how bad gays had it in past centuries, some of the things that had been done to them. When she got to the chapter about some of the 'treatments' that had been performed in the past, she stopped harping about me going to a doctor. Eventually, she sort of got used to the idea and stopped worrying about it. Then I brought home Shar, and… it was just awful. She sounded a lot like Rick did just now. Called him an animal, said I really was sick. She couldn't see how wonderful he is, what an amazing person. All she saw was the black fur and those big-ass ears. And I love him, but, man, he does have the biggest freaking ears I ever saw."

Fearyn laughed in agreement. "All the better to hear you with, my dear."

Liam laughed. "Yes, and let's not forget the teeth. So I admit, he's not human. But he's a kind, loving intelligent person and very important to me. I love him, fur, fleas, and all. I wish she could just be happy for me."

"Ah," said Fearyn, "I see we come at last to what is really bothering you."

Liam shook his head. "You're over-simplifying, but okay, yes. I wish I could just take my lover home with me when I go to see my family without it being a disaster. He's special to me. And I'm angry I had to choose between Christmas with my mom or Christmas with Shar. And I'm absolutely furious with myself that I let her make me choose and that I left him home alone so I could waste what used to be my favorite holiday with a group of… bigots."

"I'm sure Shar was all right. Christmas is not exactly a Khalzi holiday."

"That's not the point! I should have been home with my lover, not stuck at a table with my mom staring at me with an expression like a depressed basset hound, getting drunk and saying, 'My poor, poor baby, someone did something so horrible to you.' And my brother with that bitch of a wife of his barking at me, and Dad demanding to know how I could do this to the family. I should have been home with Shar, watching Christmas specials and trying to explain the significance of the dead evergreen in the corner being humiliated."

Fearyn burst out laughing, having asked that question of his friend years ago. Liam grinned despite himself and tossed away the remains of his cigarette. They walked together in silence for a little while, their footsteps echoing quietly down the dark street.

"There's always next year," said Fearyn softly.

Liam suddenly stopped in his tracks. Fearyn paused as well, looking at his friend. He raised an eyebrow and smiled.

"You look as if you have just had an epiphany."

Liam looked towards Fearyn. "Let's celebrate Christmas."

"I thought Christmas was over."

"Yeah, it is, but why can't we do it again?"

"I beg your pardon?"

Liam was more and more delighted with his idea. "Sure! Why can't the four of us have Christmas together? You and Faunnis and me and Shar. Snow and a tree and carols and turkey and gifts…"

"Liam, this is Sferkkaa. It does not snow here. Rain, yes, snow, no."

"I have a cabin on Earth, in the mountains. I was thinking about selling it because I seldom use it anymore, but… I don't think I will now."

Fearyn raised an eyebrow. "So, just the four of us, in the middle of nowhere?"

"It'll be perfect!"

"You don't think, for one moment, you are going to get Shar out in the snow."

"Stranger things have happened. So are you with me?"

"Of course, it's a brilliant chance to study the intricacies of an alien culture. Besides, I'm dying to see you get Shar outside making snowmen. Or snow-Khalzi."

"I'm sure I can persuade him. And I get to live out every kid's wildest fantasy." He grinned at Fearyn. "Second Christmas."

* * *

Liam said good night to Fearyn in the hallway and then quietly unlocked the door to his own hotel room. He stepped inside, pocketing the room key, then turned and smiled at the being on the bed.

Rick had been accurate when he compared Khalzi to Anubis. In fact, the similarities were far too close to be a coincidence, though not even the most meticulous of space historians and archaeologists could find evidence Khalzi had ever come to Earth. Shar was lounging on the bed, reading. In one hand, he had a book, and in the other, a partly melted chocolate. The short whiskers at the end of his long muzzle were perked forward, which they always did when he was engrossed in something. The tall, erect ears were forward as well, and the heavy, golden hair that began between the large ears fell in a heavy curtain around his shoulders and down his chest. His frame was long and slender, powerful and well muscled, yet light: the body of a dancer or swimmer. He was covered all over in very short, very black, very silky fur that always reminded Liam of a cropped rabbit fur coat his favorite aunt, Helen, used to own. But Shar was softer and warmer.

109

Shar finally recalled his melting chocolate and ate it, then idly sucked the remains off his long, elegant fingers. Liam's eyes narrowed, and he felt his jeans begin to get tight. He walked over to the bed and plucked the book from Shar's hand.

"What say we put on The Bangles' 'Walk Like an Egyptian' and do naughty things to each other?"

Shar's large ears directed traffic. "I was reading that, mortal. Do not make me scoop your brains out with a hook."

"You can read anytime. Let's play Little Red Riding Hood. You can be Red."

Shar rolled his eyes. "You're a pervert, you realize." He moved closer to Liam, snuggling against him, his head on his chest. He could smell the unmistakable stink of beer and cigarettes. "Did you and Fearyn enjoy yourselves?"

"Well… yes and no. You'll never guess who was in the pub. Rick."

The ears flattened. Liam ran his hand over them, smiling faintly.

"I didn't know he would be there, believe me. If I had, I would have stayed here. He's blind now, and he lost that arm you stripped. You know, I was hoping it would have made him wake up and do something about how he was living his life, but if anything, he's worse. It was the same old crap, just more so. Nothing is his fault, and even if it is his fault, it's still not his fault. Someone made him do it."

"I'm sure he had a few choice words about me."

Liam nodded. "Oh, yeah. Bastard. I can't, for the life of me, see what I saw in him. I must have been out of my mind." He looked down at Shar and smiled, unable to resist scratching him behind the ears. "Glad to see my taste has improved."

"Well, your brother David doesn't think so. He called and left a message. You're invited to his wife's birthday party on February first. Oh, and it's a pet-free event. Then he repeated the message using barks and growls."

Liam felt a sudden, violent rage. Reaching out he snatched up the phone and dialed, knowing it would take at least thirty minutes for the call to travel from Sferkkaa to Earth and hoping he didn't calm down in the meantime. At last, he reached his brother's voice mail.

"Hello, David? It's Liam. Very funny, asshole. By the way, your bitch wife is fucking both your friend Stewart and your friend Andrew. Happy fucking New Year, shitwad."

He slammed the phone down so hard, he briefly feared he had broken the thing. Then he stood up and began packing. Shar sat up, alarmed.

"Where are you going?"

Liam packed, then walked over to his lover. His beautiful, beautiful lover, with the long gold hair and warm brown eyes, like pools of dark chocolate swirled with caramel. He touched his face, feeling his rage slowly leave him.

"I want to do something for you. For me, too."

"You're not going to kill David, are you?"

"Much as I would like to, no. I'm going to go to the cabin on Earth. Tomorrow night, Fearyn and Faunnis are going to bring you there, and the four of us are going to spend some time far away from the Ricks and Davids of the world."

"What are we going to do?"

Liam grinned. "Second Christmas." He kissed the soft muzzle. "I love you. I'll see you tomorrow night."

Liam picked up his bag and left the room, leaving Shar alone to wonder what his lover was up to.

* * *

Liam used his own private planet hopper to head back to Earth. A planet hopper was a small craft, not much larger than a fighter jet. It could hold a crew of three, or a family of seven if someone happened to have a can of axel grease and a shoehorn. Liam bought his from the base he was stationed at when this particular model was declared obsolete. However, it was still a good little craft, and he had taken endless delight in painting it silk black and decorating it with ancient Egyptian symbols. The planet hopper's name was, not surprisingly, Anubis, a name to which it had been programmed to respond.

He landed it in the parking lot of a shopping mall, much to the annoyance of the motorists who had hoped to use the parking spaces the wings now occupied, and to the extreme delight of the children in the cars with them. Liam grinned and walked into the mall, ignoring the irritated screech of tires behind him.

He returned to his craft about an hour later, loaded down with three shopping carts full of stuff.

Christmas shopping was so much more enjoyable after Christmas. He reached his little planet hopper, humming Christmas carols, finding it surrounded by excited children and amused adults. Liam suddenly realized with a sigh that someone, probably Fearyn, had reprogrammed the verbal warnings the craft's alarm system would utter.

Instead of a calm and soft "Please do not touch the vehicle," Liam instead heard "Hey! Piss off. Keep your hands away; this paint is new. Hey! I saw that. I have photon torpedoes, and I am *not* afraid to use them."

Liam sighed. "Anubis, stand down."

"Oh! Come crawling back, have we? Well, forget it. I'm not speaking to you. Leaving me out here all alone."

Liam grit his teeth. "Anubis, stand down."

"No. Not until you confirm your identity."

Liam sighed and held up his hand for the plane to scan his handprint. The plane scanned, then said, "Buttocks not recognized."

"Open the hell up!"

"Password recognized. Greetings, Liam."

Liam growled, then muttered, "Just wait, Fearyn. Your own hopper is about to learn to sing like those yodeling cowboys in the old black and white movies."

"Your plane's funny!" said a small girl.

"Thank you," said Liam. "Now I'm going to have to find my friend's plane and make it funny for him."

The child's father chuckled at the idea. Liam loaded everything into the hopper, most of which he stowed in wing compartments meant for carrying bombs and ammunition. It was only eight in the morning, but he had a lot to do before Shar, Fearyn, and Faunnis arrived.

* * *

He was starting to understand why his mother always seemed pissed off Christmas Eve.

He cut down a tree and hauled it into the cabin, then got a fire started and turned on some carols to get him in the mood. He put the tree in the stand, then went to get the turkey ready. He made stuffing, then prepared a few pumpkin pies, which went in at the same time as the turkey so they would be ready in plenty of time to cool. He started decorating the room and then realized he'd forgotten to buy tree ornaments. Recalling the beautiful ornaments left by his aunt in the attic, he went up to find they had all been destroyed by raccoons. It smelled like raccoons. Disgusting beasts. There wasn't an animal alive he hated more than raccoons. So back to the mall for ornaments and a few other odds and ends and back to the cabin he went. He returned in time to realize he had forgotten the pies in the oven. They were now burned.

Oh, yeah, he was getting the holiday spirit all right. He opened a bottle of orange brandy and started over.

* * *

It had, without a doubt, been one of the most infuriating days of his life, but by the time the turkey was ready and Shar was due to arrive, the place was perfect. The tree was up and decorated, the fire was lit, and the room smelled of spice and wine. The table was laid, the stockings were hung, the gifts were wrapped, and Charles Dickens himself could not have done better. It had even begun to snow. Liam stood in the living room, staring out over the snow, basking in the glorious warmth and beauty of the lights and the fire. It was all so wonderful; he could just stand there forever.

He was broken out of his peaceful reverie by the sight of not one planet hopper arriving, but three. One was definitely Alloicious, which was Fearyn's craft, but he did know the other two. He watched Fearyn and Faunnis hop out of their plane and try to talk someone out of it, while the other two craft unloaded what looked like…

Liam suddenly bolted out of the house and into the falling snow. He laughed in surprise and joy. "Sherry! Oh, my god, Sherry, it's been six years!"

"Almost seven," she replied. "And you have the Sferkkaan Armed Forces to thank for landing in my yard on Alcardia Three, scaring the hell out of me and kidnapping me to see you."

Liam leapt on his favorite cousin and hugged her, then pounced on her husband to hug him, too. "Brendan! Missed you! Jesus, where did all these kids come from? Sherry, there's seven of them!"

"Well, only four of them are mine, the other three belong to my friend Diane, but she's sick right now, so I have them. Besides, I thought they could use a second Christmas as well. They didn't have a very happy one what with Mommy ill and dearest Daddy… well… we can talk about that later. Here.”

She passed him a bag. Liam took it and opened it, and felt a cold fear go through himself.

“Aw, Sherry, no, please, you can’t be serious, don’t make me do it! What about Brendan?”

“The kids will know it’s him, and before you suggest Fearyn or Faunnis, no! Santa Claus does not wear makeup.”

“He does on Sferkkaa.”

“He does,” said Faunnis. “I used to date him.”

Sherry rolled her eyes. “Please, we all know Santa has been happily married to Mrs. Clause for many, many years, and no matter what either of them may do on the side, we do not discuss it in front of the kids.” Sherry fixed her favorite cousin with laughing green eyes. “Right, Santa?”

“I hate you. You’re not really my cousin, you know. You’re adopted.”

“Just help me get the presents out of this nice man’s hopper before he’s AWOL from his base.”

“I wish I’d known you were coming. I would have got something for the kids.”

“You did. I sent Brendan out and told him to think like a jarhead.”

“I am not a jarhead. Marines are jarheads. I am a member of His Imperial Highness’ Royal Air Force.”

“So you’re an airhead.”

“You’re adopted, and your real parents are in prison.”

“So that’s why I keep getting letters from the penitentiary.”

They unloaded the hoppers, and the pilots were off almost before Liam could thank them. Then he walked over to Alloicious, smiling as he leaned inside, looking down into a pair of nervous dark eyes, the tall ears back in a worried position.

"It's not dangerous, you know," said Liam.

Shar's ears did strange things as their owner surveyed the falling snow. "I've never seen it. To tell you the truth, I thought it was just a story."

Liam smiled, reaching in to touch his lover's face. "Nope. It's real. Coming inside?"

Shar looked nervous. He watched the children shrieking and playing, pelting Sherry, Brendan, Faunnis, and Fearyn with snowballs.

"Perhaps I'll just go inside." Liam smiled. "We can do that."

Shar smiled. It looked odd with his jackal face, but it was definitely a smile. He opened his jacket, and a small head poked out.

Liam sighed. "Shar, what is that?"

"It's my brother's baby."

"Shar…"

"I wanted her here. It has nothing at all to do with trying to talk you into starting a family. Nothing at all."

Liam sighed and picked the baby up. She was about a year old, a tiny bundle in a little pink dress with matching boots and mittens. She was too young for her ears to have formed properly yet, so they lay flat, like a rabbit's. She would be five before they stood erect. She had the end of her tail in her mouth, the

Khalzi version of thumb sucking. Liam sighed again and watched his tall leggy lover exit the hopper.

"You're incorrigible, you know it. And think how my mom and brother will be if they ever found out you had one in the pouch."

"So who are you living for?" said Shar. "Them or yourself? Why is it our problem they choose to be bigoted fools?"

Shar was right, of course. Liam looked down at the little bundle of black and pink in his arms. She was awfully, nearly painfully, cute.

"Come on, let's get her inside. It's cold."

Shar nodded, and they began walking towards the cabin.

"Dinner in half an hour," Liam called to the rampaging hoard of children. "Then early bed so Second Santa can come."

The mention of Second Santa elicited shrieks of approval from the kids, and the baby Khalzi hid beneath Liam's jacket, frightened by the outcry. He held her close, and they walked into the soft, beautiful light of the cabin. Shar gasped quietly, eyes large, his nose working as he tried to sort all the scents and sights.

"It is all so very beautiful! Oh, what is that smell?"

"Turkey and stuffing, sausage gravy, onion bread, stuffed mushrooms, and pumpkin pie."

Shar breathed in all the wonderful scents, then looked at Liam and smiled. "This was a brilliant idea."

Liam smiled. "Yeah, I was actually thinking of making it a tradition."

"I think we should."

Liam leaned close and kissed Shar's face. His one regret that this simple act was the only one a Khalzi could not do. He passed him the baby.

"I'll be right back. I have one last thing to do."

Liam went to the closet and pulled out an old full-length coat of cropped rabbit fur. It still smelled of his aunt's favorite perfume, though the scent was becoming faint now and musty. He remembered snuggling into this coat in this very cabin on Christmas Eve, waiting for Santa, but always falling asleep just before he came. He carried the coat into the living room and spread it on the floor before the tree. He then took the baby and set her down on it, smiling as she immediately pulled a candy cane down from the branches. Liam put an arm around Shar.

"Correct me if I'm wrong, but you don't have a brother. And... she doesn't seem to have a name."

Shar stared at Liam with those intense brown eyes. "We could give her one. A Second Christmas present."

"Where did she come from?"

"She was found in a smuggler's ship, in a crate in the hold. She was covered in blood, probably her father's. The team that went out to apprehend the ship didn't know what to do with her, so they brought her back to the base. We bathed her, and one of the Sferkkaan officers had the little pink outfit left over from her own daughter. She gave it to her."

Liam sighed heavily. "I have to hand it to you, Shar. You not only get what you want, you make sure you have guilt enough to keep me from arguing about it."

"So we can keep her?"

"Well, I'd have to be a bloody ogre to send her away after that! Fine. We can keep her."

Shar leapt on him, holding him tightly, wrapping his long legs around his waist. Liam laughed.

"Of course, you know that means you have to marry me."

Shar froze and raised his head to look at Liam. "Oh, Liam, you know very well Khalzi don't marry. We're a nomadic race, and males and females generally don't stay together, although there have been exceptions…"

"Well, what kind of parents would we be if we let that poor little sad nameless baby grow up without her daddy and daddy properly married?"

Shar's ears flattened. "That's not fair, using my own tactics against me."

"Is that a yes?"

"Yes. And I love you."

"I love you, too. Now you go help her get the candy cane out of her fur while I start laying dinner on the table."

Chapter 10: Sleep Walk with Me

Mick Blamires walked quietly through the autumn wood, his powerful crossbow slung comfortably in his arm, and he savored the smell of the woods. Deer hunting had long been a passion of his, one taught to him by his father and older sister. However, the point of the hunt, as far as Mick was concerned, was never to actually bag a deer so much as it was to have an excuse to spend a few days tramping in the woods. He paused and breathed deep of the cool air, the sweet scent of maple leaves in their fall colours. He felt a pang of loneliness as he thought of his father and sister, wishing they were still with him. They had died three years ago, killed when their car was sideswiped on an icy road by a drunk. His mother had passed away twelve years earlier of a heart condition.

He was alone in the world, but somehow, when he was out among the trees, he did not feel alone. He thought he could feel their spirits walking with him. Sometimes, he even thought he could hear his sister laughing as their father once again misfired his medieval weapon. His father was a terrible shot with a bow, but it never stopped him from trying. The woods had been a very large and happy part of his childhood, and now, as an adult, they still gave him peace of mind and spirit. He breathed deeply once more, closing his eyes, savouring the autumnal forest.

"I could live here," he said softly.

He heard a curse from behind him and sighed. Turning, he looked at the man accompanying him. His business partner Thomas Richards was sliding down a slight embankment, his hunting rifle at a dangerous angle. The fool was going to blow his own head off.

"Careful, Tommy! Don't do anything I don't want to explain to the paramedics!"

Thomas swore. "I'm fine!" he snapped and got up.

Mick watched Thomas get up and brush the forest debris off himself. He shook his head, sighed, then noticed a brown rabbit calmly staring at him. He winked at the beast.

"And a very good day to you, Master Bunny. You'll be pleased to know I'm only bothering the deer today."

The rabbit watched him as he set down his crossbow and removed his small pack. He placed this down on the forest floor and opened it, taking out a blue ceramic dish. The plate was plainly of great age and bore a design of Celtic origin, featuring running stags. He set it upon a stump, then reached into his bag again and took out a finger of hand-churned butter. Next, he took out a glass bottle of cream and set it beside the butter. He glanced up at the bunny once more, then pulled out a piece of apple and carefully tossed it to the furry brown animal. He straightened, hearing Thomas come to stand by him.

"What's that for?" asked Thomas.

"For the Good Folk," said Mick.

Thomas' tone was questioning. "'Good Folk?'"

Mick repacked his bag, leaving the cream and butter on the plate. "You, I believe, would call them Elves. But never call them Faeries. They hate that."

Thomas stared at his business partner of eight years with utter disbelief on his face. "You are joking me."

"No, I'm not."

"Since when have you started believing in hippie-dippy new age bull?"

Mick sighed heavily. "Thomas, my mother was a proud Irishwoman, and she taught me a lot about the ways of the Good Folk and the Spirit Realm. And just because I am in Canada, I see no reason not to show respect and leave a traditional offering."

"Nothing's going to eat that but a fox."

Mick shrugged. "Be that as it may."

"And there's no such things as Elves."

"If it pleases you to think that."

Thomas snorted, and Mick just shook his head. Thomas was very much rooted in what he liked to call reality. That was what made him so good at business and such a terrible pain in the arse. But Mick was not a man who judged. Besides, he rather liked the old crank. He glanced at the man beside him. Thomas was thin, harried, and balding, with a blood pressure level that gave his doctor palpitations. He was basically a good soul but had been born without a sense of humour and no idea of how to relax. So Mick had invited him deer hunting, and, to his utter surprise, Thomas accepted.

"I can't believe you think this is fun," cranked Thomas.

"I can't believe I thought it was a good idea to invite you."

"So we're even." Thomas paused and drew breath. "Mick, I have to talk to you."

Mick had been friends with Thomas long enough to recognize the tone of his voice. He nodded, and the two seated themselves on the ground. Thomas lit a cigarette, which Mick ignored. The brown bunny chewed the piece of apple and watched the men.

"What is it, Tommy?"

Thomas fixed Mick with a glare as he shook his match, dumping the now-cool stick of wood into his pocket. He did not appreciate being addressed as 'Tommy' by a thirty-year-old man who looked like a twenty-year-old kid and whose long, heavy mane of red hair was begging for a cut.

"It's Cinnamon."

"Oh, what about Cinnamon?" said Mick, his tone exasperated. Some days, it seemed like all Thomas and Cinnamon did was snipe at each other.

Mick had met Cinnamon a year ago, and it had been love at first sight, or at the very least, lust. She had long, auburn hair, and full breasts, which pressed wantonly against the thin fabric of her black lace shirt. He was pretty sure she was not standing on that street corner in hopes that a Bible reading would break out, but she seemed genuinely glad of his company. She was homeless and living behind a dumpster, and Mick could not leave her to her fate. Certainly, her tight little ass fighting against the confines of her short leather skirt had something to do with it, but Mick was, by nature, a man who could not leave people to their misery. Over time, he made friends with her, took her to a doctor, paid to have her teeth fixed after a john tried to knock them out, and finally gave her a job in one of his stores. He sold camping, hunting, and fishing equipment, which she knew nothing about. Yet, somehow, she was the best salesperson he had.

Plainly, this was due to her enthusiasm for outdoor sports, thought Mick wryly.

She had moved in with him six months ago, and ever since, they had been talking marriage and family. He bought her a little red sports car, a three-carat diamond engagement ring, and hired a contractor to add onto his house, to create rooms for the family that was to follow. She bought for him a huge band of platinum and diamonds, which he was currently wearing, as a promissory ring. It did not matter that she had used his money to do it; he was just pleased she thought of him.

Life was perfect and beautiful. Except for one slight detail. Thomas and Cinnamon could not stand each other and never seemed to tire of biting pieces out of each other.

This time, however, Thomas did not bite. He reached into his own rucksack and pulled out a book, which Mick recognized as their accounts ledger. Thomas was deeply distrustful of computers.

"You took that thing hunting?" asked Mick with disbelief.

Thomas tossed the book into Mick's lap. "Your little boy-toy is a thief."

"Bull," said Mick. "She's not smart enough. And I say that with love."

"Uh huh."

Mick opened the book and began looking through it. Slowly, he read through the ledger, noting the numbers that had been erased and re-written in another denomination in a poor impersonation of Thomas' Headmaster script.

"Pretty baby has been into the candy jar," said Thomas dryly.

"How long have you known?"

"Few months, but I know how you feel about Cinnamon. Not that I approve, mind, but I don't go meddling in anyone's relationship without just cause."

Mick shook his head, feeling his stomach churn as his heart broke and his eyes began to burn. Page after page after page it went on – a hundred dollars here, two hundred there. A slight change of a number, a little out of the till, and thousands upon thousands of dollars were being siphoned off. Finally, he slammed the book shut.

"Damn! How could she do that to me, after everything I have done for her! She was living in a dumpster for fuck sakes! I take her in, give her a job, a home, my love! And *this* is the thanks I get?"

Thomas looked uncomfortable. "I'm sorry," he said.

"So am I," said Mick.

He brought his hands up over his eyes, gritting his teeth, feeling his heart shatter into a thousand pieces. His life, his whole life, and all his dreams had just been destroyed. He felt himself beginning to shake, and he gasped once, fighting the need to cry out like an animal in pain. Anger began to creep in under the hurt, and he welcomed it. He lowered his hands, and found, to his astonishment, that the wild rabbit was now in his lap. He carefully stroked its soft fur, gently playing with the long, velvety ears. Then he looked at Thomas.

"Is this why you said you would go out hunting with me? To show me this?"

Thomas shrugged. "Oh, that, and one other reason."

"What would that be?"

There came the distinct sound of a rifle being cocked off to his right, and Mick went cold. He slowly turned his head and saw his beautiful lover of the last six months. Cinnamon was dressed in denim and leather, hardly proper attire for the woods. The way the blue fabric clung to her thighs made Mick wish he was an inseam. Thomas sat back with a smug grin on his face, while Cinnamon stared at Mick with eyes utterly devoid of emotion.

"I'm afraid I'm also fucking your partner, dear," said Cinnamon.

The explosion sent the wild rabbit fleeing for his life. Mick fell heavily to the ground, blood draining through the hole in his chest. The world went dark and silent. As Thomas and Cinnamon left him, a few gentle leaves fluttered down, as though expressing concern and sadness for the mortally injured man. The last thought Mick had was that he hoped they did not smash his mother's blue dish.

* * *

Am I awake?

Mick thought he smelled wood smoke, but he couldn't be sure. He seemed to recall that severe head injuries could cause all sorts of bizarre side effects. No, he had been shot in the chest. His head was fine.

Hospital, he thought. *Must get to a hospital, find help. How can I get out of the woods?*

Mick pushed at the ground with one hand, trying to lift his maimed body. The leaves seemed to have been replaced with a smooth, yielding surface, one that gave pleasantly beneath his hand. He opened his eyes and found he was lying on a bed. The surface was a mattress covered by a sheet of rough-woven cotton.

He looked around the room, studying the walls of fragrant cedar wood and the stone floor. There was a hearth in one wall, made of fieldstones, a small fire burning within. Over the fire hung an iron kettle, and its contents steamed, filling the room with the smell of tea. Before the hearth lay a rug of deer skin. In the corner to the left of the hearth was a rustic chair of wood and wicker, and on it sat a man.

He was tall and slender, his aristocratic face thin, with high, cutting cheekbones. His skin was white and utterly flawless, the nose long and straight. His lips were red, unnaturally so, and the long black hair hung straight, falling past his narrow shoulders. His long, elegant hands were folded on his lap, and he wore a black robe that pooled on the floor around his feet, looking almost like the base of a tree, as though the garment somehow gave him a connection to the earth beneath him. The eyes were black as well, and depthless, like pits into another universe. They did not blink but watched Mick with a cold, regal expression. Every millimeter of this man exuded power and nobility, strength untold, hidden within his placid countenance. Mick knew, the same way he knew that the sun would rise and the sky was blue, that this was no man.

This was an Elf.

Not the cheerful little Santa's helpers of childhood stories, not the golden and wise creatures of Tolkien's renowned tales, but a creature of great age and power. This was the being the Irish whispered tales about in their pubs and refused to cross under any circumstances. This was a wild thing of a capricious nature, one who could either be kind and helpful, or very, very dangerous. Mick tried desperately to recall everything his mother had told him about Elves on those long-ago nights when he would sit on her knee. His father had not believed but was pleased his wife was passing on her myths and heritages to her children. Indeed, his father enjoyed the tales himself. But his mother had been dead these past fifteen years, and his knowledge of the Good Folk had grown thin.

He swallowed nervously, determined to show this creature every courtesy he was due. He opened his mouth to speak, but the Elf was no longer paying attention to him. He rose to his feet, moving with silent grace. Mick estimated his height at around seven feet and, despite himself, let his eyes run down the being's long, curved back, admiring the black silken hair. Then he shook his head, surprised at finding himself gazing at another male in such a way.

The Elf poured them each a cup of tea, then turned and walked to the bed, seating himself on the edge. He offered Mick a cup, and Mick took it, bowing his head.

"Thank you," he said softly and sipped it, remembering as he did so that one should not eat or drink the food of the Good Folk. *Screw it*, he thought, *chances are I'm dead anyway.* He cleared his throat.

"Thank you for helping me."

The Elf watched him coolly, likely still making up his mind about the mere mortal before him. Mick did not press. Elf and man drank their tea in silence. When the last drops were drained from their cups, Mick happened to notice his clothes, folded neatly on a chest beside the bed. He was very certain that neither the chest nor clothes had been there a moment ago. Lying atop the clothes was the most stunningly beautiful longbow he had ever seen. It was crafted of yew and filigreed with running stags and the repeating Celtic knot. He dared not guess at what it was strung with, but it did not look like anything with which he was familiar.

"Such a lovely bow," he said. "Is it yours?"

The Elf spoke, his voice touched with an accent that could only be Irish. "Surely, it is yours, sir."

Mick broke into a sweat. Was it a gift? Or was this a test? A wrong answer could have some truly negative effects. "Mine?"

"Indeed, it has lain here beside you all this time, so yours it must be. Do you not know your own things?"

Mick swallowed, trying desperately to recall the delicate word play required for speaking with mystical beings. His business college had been sadly lacking on the subject. He decided the bow must be a gift.

"Oh, yes, I recognize it now. So very lovely it is, and so finely made. Only an artisan of great skill could have made such a bow."

The Elf seemed pleased, although his expression did not change.

Mick sensed he had made the proper response.

"I am Mick," he said.

This time, the Elf did seem to smile, though the expression was restrained, as though he was reminding himself not to get too familiar with strange humans.

"You may call me Llewellyn."

Mick took careful note of the phrasing. Not 'I am Llewellyn,' but 'You may call me Llewellyn.' After all, no self-respecting being of the Hidden World gave his true name to just anyone.

"I am most pleased and thankful to be given the hospitality of your home."

"As well you should be. You know what I am, do you not?"

Mick nodded. "Indeed, I do." He swallowed, feeling odd as he uttered the next two words. "My lord."

"I should have left you to your fate, but I was most intrigued to find one in this land who knows the traditional offerings to beg safe passage from us."

"My mother hailed from Limerick. She did her best to teach me."

"She was wise to do so, for it saved your life. Do all men treat each other thusly?"

Mick shook his head. "No," he whispered, feeling his eyes burn as he thought of the depth of the betrayal he had suffered. "I, for one, would never do such a thing."

The Elf tilted his head to one side, seeming to express sympathy. "Sleep," whispered Llewellyn, and Mick did, lying back against the pillow and closing his eyes mere moments after the uttering of the word.

* * *

When next he opened his eyes, the sun was shining, and he could hear birds trilling. The door to the simple chamber was open, and he could feel a gentle autumn wind blowing through the little stone house.

He looked down at his chest and saw a ghastly wound that made him sick to look at. The outer edges were burned and ragged, tattooed with speckles of unburned gunpowder, and small holes where shot had lodged in his flesh. The center was black and oozing blood, but it did not seem to be much more than a flesh wound. Either Llewellyn had healing capabilities beyond that of any doctor, or the shot had somehow misfired, leaving him bleeding and abraded but alive.

Somehow, Mick did not think the shot had gone awry.

He slid out of bed and dressed in his clothes. They were dirty and bloody, and Mick did not think that was an accident either. No, he felt that the Elf knew he had to go back to confront those who had betrayed him, and he would need evidence.

He gathered up his few things, noting with a smile that his blue plate was in his bag. Lastly, he

132

picked up the gorgeous longbow that Llewellyn had given him and walked out of the little stone house.

The yard surrounding it was of natural moss and small wildflowers, and, not far away, stood Llewellyn in his long black robe, gazing at him with serene, unblinking eyes.

Mick grinned like a fool at the Elf, unable to contain himself. He did not know why, but the very sight of him was like salve to his physical and emotional wounds. Llewellyn raised an eyebrow and looked away, pretending to be miffed with such an unseemly display. Mick walked up to him, and the pair began strolling through the woods.

"You must depart now," said Llewellyn. It was not a question.

"I understand." Mick glanced at the tall Elf. "Will I see you again? Or, should I say, may I see you again?"

"And why should I wish to be seen by so mere a creature as you?"

Mick didn't have an answer to that. He only knew that a piece of himself found great comfort in the Elf's presence, but he did not think the Elf would be impressed by this. He fell silent, walking alongside Llewellyn. After a few minutes, Llewellyn spoke.

"You may see me again, if you wish."

Mick almost hopped with glee but stopped himself. "Thank you."

"But answer me this. Why should you wish to come see me? You know what I am, you know that I am no gentle children's myth."

"I do," said Mick softly. "But you… you fascinate me. I long to hear you speak of your life, and I desire to sit at your feet and gaze upon you as you speak and wonder what mystic things your ancient eyes have seen."

Llewellyn seemed pleased and a little flattered. "Then you must bring me a gift."

Mick felt some part of himself bridle at the statement. Faery creatures were wont to request some pretty outrageous things, and he was having mental images of himself driving all over Vancouver, seeking the breath of a fish or some such thing.

"If it is within my power, I shall."

Llewellyn smiled. "Ink."

"Ink?"

"And quills. I am out."

"Ink and quills I shall bring." He smiled. "Perhaps a nice computer with Photoshop and a colour printer?"

Llewellyn smiled. "Ink. And quills. You distrust my magic, I distrust yours." He looked at Mick with wise, serene, eternal eyes. "What shall you do with your faithless lover and partner?"

"I don't know yet," said Mick softly. He smiled sadly, feeling the hurt once more catch hold of him like panther claws. "I loved them both so much. I had this… foolish idea about marrying Cinnamon and having some children. The perfect little family, with Uncle Thomas over for dinner on Sundays. I am such a fool."

"You are not a fool," said Llewellyn softly. "Even I have fallen prey to faithless love. It is not a trial only mortal men must endure. We who dwell in the Green Realm feel its sting also."

"Then I name the one who hurt you a fool," said Mick softly, "for only one lacking wit and heart and sense of wonder would hurt a being as very, very wonderful and lovely as you."

Llewellyn paused and looked at the man, as though surprised a mortal would dare say such a thing. Mick was a little surprised himself, wondering where the feelings welling up in his battered chest were coming from. Gratitude, he supposed, and a muddle of other emotions he had no words for. The pair stared at each other, then Llewellyn regained his Elven decorum.

"Your beast awaits you."

Mick turned, and grinned at the sight of his red SUV, waiting like some faithful hound. Cinnamon must have followed in her own vehicle. He looked back towards Llewellyn, once more caught up in his black eyes. He was still astonished at himself, but he was getting used to the attraction he felt for this being. His male sensibilities comforted him by saying he did not want the Elf; he was simply curious about him.

"May I touch you?" he asked softly.

Llewellyn's expression hovered between amused and outraged.

Fortunately, amusement won out.

"You may."

Mick reached up one hand and carefully, lightly, touched one fine cheekbone. His flesh was cold, but not in the way a dead animal was. He was cold like stone and running water and ice melting from a tree limb. It was a beautiful, natural cold, and somehow oddly fitting. He next touched the long hair, cold also and slick, like strands of something more fair and fine than silk.

The two gazed at each other. Then Mick stepped back, suddenly feeling like a child who has overstepped his bounds.

"Until we meet again," he said softly.

Llewellyn inclined his head in agreement, then turned and walked back into the deep woods, still in his black robe, his passing disturbing no twig or leaf. Then he was gone.

* * *

Mick drove for hours in a strange state of suspended animation, his body working independent of his will and mind. He followed the long road like some sort of homing device, his actions automatic. He pulled into his driveway at long last, uncertain as to how many hours he had been driving but not surprised at the presence of police cars. No doubt Cinnamon and Thomas were weeping out their tale about how deeply worried they were for their dear, dear friend.

Mick slowly got out of his vehicle, his movements shaky, his eyes glazed. He was feeling the severity of his injury as he walked slowly up the gravel drive, hearing the stones crunch beneath his feet, smelling the sweet fall air. It was close to evening, and the world was becoming dark and cold as the sky faded to purple.

He quietly entered his house, closing the door behind himself, hearing muffled voices in the living room down the hall. He walked towards it, finding himself unusually interested in the three high windows that made up the far wall of the large room he staggered into. He continued into the room, still gazing at the windows, thinking of black eyes that had seen the dawn of time and had looked upon things he could never hope to see.

The room became silent. The two police officers stood, silent and horrified at the state of him. Thomas made a small, frightened cry, and Cinnamon just stared, certain her eyes must be playing tricks on her. Mick slowly drew his gaze away from the windows and looked towards the policemen. The ledger was in his hands, though he did not remember carrying it with him into the house.

"I don't know what they told you," he said quietly, "but they tried to kill me. They've also been embezzling from my company." He held up the ledger. "I have proof."

Thomas looked at Cinnamon, who was staring cold daggers of hate at Mick. Listlessly, Mick passed the closest officer the book, then slumped down into a chair. He heard nothing more as Thomas and Cinnamon were arrested, and the ambulance summoned.

* * *

Mick was sick for a long time.

The wounds were dirty, and they had infected. From what he heard, however, through his fever and illness, he was lucky to even be alive. The injury caused by the shotgun should have killed him. Sometimes, he could hear the doctors quietly arguing

137

about what had kept him alive and how on earth a man in his condition had driven the nine hours it took him to get home.

"Someone was watching over him, that's for sure," said one young doctor. The others felt compelled to agree. There was no reason for Mick to still be alive.

He languished in the hospital a long time, his body fighting the infection that ravaged it. The staff were kind to him. No doubt the doctors and nurses felt a great deal of sympathy for this man who had been horribly betrayed and now had no one to sit with him as he fought for his life. Twice, the policemen who had arrested Cinnamon and Thomas came to visit, sitting with him briefly, telling him what had become of the pair. Cinnamon, it seemed, had been wanted on warrants too numerous to recall, and the attempted murder of her lover was but one more foul deed. She would not be seeing daylight again.

Thomas had killed himself.

When Mick became stronger, he sold off his business and most of his other assets. He could have comfortably lived off the proceeds for the rest of his life, but his old dreams now seemed faded and uninteresting. Especially since most of them had involved Cinnamon and his offspring and Sunday dinners with Uncle Thomas. Dreams that would haunt him and play over and over in his mind as he sat in his favorite chair in his beautiful house.

He went to visit her once, feeling small and sick as he entered the cold, imposing penitentiary, but she would not see him. She was still miffed over what he had done to her.

"What I did to her?" said Mick to the female guard, not knowing if he was amused or outraged. "What, you mean survive her attempt to blow a hole in me and steal everything I had?"

The guard shrugged and gave him a tired sigh. "Yup. You're a right bastard," she said and gave him a friendly slap on the back.

He watched her as she walked away, then looked down at the wide, expensive band of precious metal and glittering gems that Cinnamon had bought for him. Even the ring seemed faded and dull.

Mick left the prison, never to return. He cursed himself for wanting to see her. He was not even certain anymore that he had ever loved her. It was hard to sort through the maelstrom of emotions to know just what he had felt. Desire certainly, sympathy, and affection, but he did not think he had loved her.

He went home, opened a bottle of wine, and seated himself in his favorite chair, staring out the windows. He did not wish to think about Cinnamon anymore, but he held his little dream close to his breast, like an abused child he needed to protect. His little faded grey dream of a family and loving home. It became a nightly ritual, and it seemed he had ceased to live and was waiting only to die.

Then, one night, as he was about to once again sit before the large window in his favorite chair and drown out the grey dreams with a bottle of good wine, he spied something resting on his leather sofa. Something beautiful and delicate, crafted with other-worldly skill, and filigreed with stags and Celtic knots.

The bow had not been there earlier, but now it sat, warm and beautiful and very real, the only brightness in his dark world. Mick recalled a promise made almost a year ago to the day. He set his glass of wine aside and picked up the bow, running his hands over it.

"Ink," he whispered. "And quills."

* * *

The next morning, Mick was up early and feeling better. The trees once more seemed golden in their fall splendor, and there was a sweetness to the air he had missed. He breathed deeply, then loaded his pack into the cab of his red SUV. Next, he placed a carefully wrapped bow inside, and finally got in himself, closing the door and starting the engine.

He drove to Granville Island, a small peninsula of land, which held an array of shops that catered to artists. He found one that sold what he desired and bought all the inks he could. Inks of gold and silver, black and red, green and yellow. Inks of all colours, and the finest quills they had to offer. The salesperson put his purchases into a box for him, and he left the shop.

He had just stepped out of the shop when movement caught his eye. He paused and smiled faintly at the two young men he saw not far away. They were rough-housing, the way young men do, pulling and pushing each other, getting one another in headlocks to administer noogies and other forms of torture. The pair shoved at each other, like Elk stags, battling for dominance. They could not have been older than twenty-three apiece, their hair long and wild, their jeans torn, their muscles strong and defined. They were both tanned, and he suspected they spent a great deal of time outdoors.

They seemed so happy and alive, brighter than the tinted and tainted world they lived in. Mick watched them, noticing the play was slowing, and they were panting. The stags had battled themselves to a standstill, and now they circled each other, bodies close, their tanned flesh gleaming softly with a fine sheen of sweat. Then, to his surprise, they pressed close and kissed, holding each other gently.

Mick felt a strange sensation in his gut, a combination of fear and other, less tangible emotions. He thought about Llewellyn and his black hair and eyes, his cold beauty. He had been telling himself he was simply fascinated by him. Indeed, who would not be fascinated by Llewellyn? He was an Elf, for Christ's sake! Only a card-carrying idiot would not be utterly captivated by him. But maybe it was not just what Llewellyn was that made Mick think of him. Maybe there was another reason as well.

Mick did not know he had approached the two men until the taller of the pair raised his head and looked at him. He had a gold nametag around his tanned throat, reading 'Nigel,' and a pair of high-top sneakers on his feet that were coming apart at the uppers.

"Learning to talk," as his mother would have said.

The slightly smaller man turned to see what had caught his lover's attention, and now both watched him, expressions wary. Nigel stroked his broad hands over his lover's shoulders, reassuring him. Mick was fairly certain they could both kick the crap out of him, but he was pretty sure Nigel would be the one to draw first blood.

Nigel stared at Mick with blue-grey eyes. When he spoke, his voice held an Australian accent. "Can we help you?" he asked, his tone suggesting he had more than his fair share in his young life of gay-bashers.

Mick felt foolish, uncertain as to what had even brought him over to the pair. He heard himself speak without knowing he was about to. "I need to ask you a question," he said quietly, "and it's probably none of my business, but, if you can tell me, I would appreciate it."

They seemed to become a little less defensive. "What do you need to know?"

Mick shifted, feeling a bit odd. He thought he may have been blushing. "When did you know you liked men?"

They seemed a little surprised by the question.

"Always," said Nigel. "Always knew." He looked at his companion. "What about you, Noel?"

"I didn't," said the other man. "I didn't know until I met this big bruiser two years ago." He gave Nigel a gentle nudge in the diaphragm with his elbow. Nigel nipped him.

"So, it would not be odd that maybe some guy didn't figure it out until he was, oh, say, thirty."

"No," said Nigel, "I don't think so. I know one guy who didn't figure it out until he was forty-seven and twenty years into a miserable marriage."

Mick flinched a bit. "Yeah, well, thankfully, I didn't have to go through that," he muttered.

He was suddenly aware of the weight of the platinum ring on his left hand, and it make him sick, like some disgusting thing that was sucking the life out of him. He pulled it off and handed the thing to Noel.

"Here," he said. "Pawn this and get your boyfriend a new pair of sneakers. His are learning to talk."

"Gold-plated sneakers," said Noel, studying the frightfully expensive trinket. Nigel peered at the ring.

"Here, are you sure you want to give this to a pair of total strangers?"

Mick looked at the pair and smiled wearily without humour. "It was supposed to be a promise of love and a future together. Seems to me you two have more use for it than I do." Then he turned and walked away, heading to his vehicle.

* * *

He drove the nine hours to the isolated location and parked his SUV. He unwrapped his bow, stringing it. He loaded the ink and quills into his pack, then, with the bow and pack, he headed into the dark forest. He walked long and far, but he did not feel himself become tired. He kept on through the night, his feet taking him along unseen paths. When dawn came, he stopped for breakfast and had a nap. Then he continued on his way.

It was just before sunset when his feet took him up a low hill that led him to a small stone cottage, surrounded by moss and small wildflowers. Mick could feel his whole spirit brighten and lift at the sight of the first mossy stone step, and by the time he reached the top of the little hill, it was as though the whole world had become bright and beautiful.

He stopped at the top of the little hill and smiled. Standing before the cottage was a tall, regal figure, clad in a black robe. Holding onto his knees were two beautiful little children, a boy and a girl, both with long red hair and large green eyes. Mick paused and looked at them as they huddled against the Elf. He did not know why, but he somehow understood that the pretty babies, who could not be more than two or three, had been abandoned and forsaken. Much like himself, they had been left in the woods to die.

He lowered his pack, walking up to face the tall, regal Elf, smiling as he felt his heart do odd things in his chest, and the butterflies awakened with a flurry in his stomach. His smile turned to a stupid grin of happiness as he realized he now understood the nature of what he felt. Llewellyn stared down his fine nose at the mortal, feigning offense. Then the little girl made a nervous whine, and the Elf's attention was drawn to the child. Mick looked down at the toddlers.

"Such lovely children," he said softly. He raised his head to look once more into the black eyes. "Are they yours?" he asked softly.

Llewellyn smiled, very faintly, his black eyes glittering playfully. "Surely they are yours, sir." His voice was equally soft.

Mick smiled and raised an eyebrow. "Mine?"

"Indeed. Do you not know your own babes?"

He stepped back and looked down at the children. "Oh, yes, I recognize them now. So very lovely they are, and so very intelligent." He knelt before the little boy and girl. "Hello."

The little girl looked at him with frightened eyes and sniffed. The little boy rubbed his nose with the back of his hand. Mick smiled at them.

"I'm your daddy."

They seemed unconvinced but looked up at Llewellyn for guidance.

"Greet your father, children," he said softly.

They did, stepping over to Mick. He picked them both up, smiling, then laughing as the little girl took an interest in his hair.

"And did you bring anything for me?" asked Llewellyn.

Mick laughed. "Beautiful ink and the finest quills, the best I could find."

"Then come in," said Llewellyn softly, "for you have been gone long, and the forest grows dark and cold."

* * *

They ate dinner together, then the children were put to bed while Mick sat in a comfortable chair on the porch, both of which had not been there when he arrived. He sighed contentedly and smiled as Llewellyn walked out of the cottage to stand beside Mick. He said nothing, but Mick could sense what he thought.

"I must leave again in the morning, mustn't I?"

Llewellyn gazed out into the night with black eyes. "Yes. For you still have ties to your world. And you must decide what it is you desire."

"I desire this," said Mick softly.

145

"You must be sure," said Llewellyn. "For you can only find this place three times, and you have already come twice. If you come again, you cannot leave."

"I do not wish to leave," said Mick softly.

Llewellyn seated himself in a chair, elegant white hands folded in his lap, staring at nothing. "You must be certain," he whispered. "For though I can give you what your heart desires, it is not easy for a mortal to dwell in our world. There are many dangers, and not all Elves tolerate Men. Indeed, I am strange among my kind, for…" He paused, debating as to whether he was revealing too much. Finally, he continued. "For I have loved a mortal before. But he shunned me. And my elder brother slew him." Llewellyn turned his head to look at Mick, his black, silky hair falling loose and soft around his white face. "I saw you leaving the gift of butter and cream, and I saw your betrayal. I was the brown rabbit you greeted. This land you are now in is an extension of your dreams, and when we are together, you are as one sleeping. We sleepwalk together in this place, and I would have you sleepwalk with me always. But as long as you have ties to your world, I cannot love you, nor can I trust you."

Mick nodded. "I understand. Then I shall leave in the morning, as you request. And I promise to return on the night of Samhain and give myself to you." He smiled.

Llewellyn smiled and looked down at his hands. He almost blushed, if such a cold beauty could do so. "Then you must bring me a gift."

Mick smiled, knowing now how this game was played.

"If it is within my power, I shall."

Llewellyn smiled. "Cloth."

"Cloth?"

"And lace. I am out."

"Cloth and lace I shall bring." He smiled. "Perhaps a nice sewing machine and serger?"

Llewellyn looked at Mick, his black eyes glittering with an affection he could not hide. "Cloth. And lace. You distrust my magic, I distrust yours."

* * *

Mick left the beautiful stone cottage, with its little stone fence, and the chickens and pony that were not there when he went to sleep. It was agony for him to depart, but he knew that Llewellyn was right. He had to be sure that this was what he wanted, and he had to know in his heart he truly wished to leave all that was familiar.

He drove back to his house, entered it, and dragged his weary body over to his favorite chair. He sat and thought. Before long, he fell asleep. And dreamed.

He dreamed of himself, in his beautiful warm house, building his new business, becoming wealthy. He saw himself meeting beautiful young women and men, loving them, disposing of them, moving on to the next. He saw himself growing old, bloated and sick on his own excess, selfish in his loneliness. He saw himself dragging his aged, broken form back to a beautiful stone cottage in the woods and weeping before the broken door that hung off its rusted hinges, the moss and wildflowers all gone. The cottage stood empty and hollow, like his life, and now it was cold and lonely, as was the man who sobbed before it, grieving the loss of true love, traded away for mere materialism.

He awoke with a jolt and reached for the phone. He knew what he had to do.

* * *

"You are certain you wish to do this?" asked Lisa.

"I am," said Mick.

The dark-haired woman sighed and shook her head. "You are a very kind man. We cannot possibly thank you for what you have done."

He smiled. "I did what I had to."

"But you are certain you wish for me to drop you off in the woods?"

"Yes."

"And what will you do there? And how do you plan to get all this cloth to where you want it?"

Mick just smiled. "I'll manage."

Lisa just shook her head and sighed again. "I wish you much happiness."

He chuckled. "Me, too."

She drove the red SUV to where he directed and stopped the vehicle. She helped him to unload the great vehicle, then stood and looked at the red-haired man before her. The man who had donated his home, vehicle, and wealth to her organization that assisted street youth and runaways.

"Thank you," she said again.

They hugged, and he watched as she got back into the vehicle and drove away. He turned and

148

grinned as he saw the pony standing patiently in its harness, hitched to a small cart. He patted the hairy little beast and loaded the lace and cloth into the cart.

"Let's go," he said to it softly and took the bridle, leading it into the woods.

* * *

It was just reaching nightfall on All Hallow's Eve when he and the cart pulled up to the little stone cottage. It was alive with coloured lanterns and lights. He could smell venison roasting and hear laughter. People he did not know stepped out of the shadows to unload the pony cart and let the little beast out of her harness. Then he turned to face the cottage and saw Llewellyn standing before him, clad in beautiful robes of forest colours, gold and red and green, a wreath of living oak ivy in his hair. Mick smiled, feeling his heart warm and the image of his old life fading away. He sighed with utter contentment and peace, ready to play the game one last time.

"Such a lovely wedding party," he said. "Is it yours?"

Llewellyn smiled, his black eyes soft and warm. "Surely, it is yours, sir."

Mick smiled and raised an eyebrow. "Mine?"

"Indeed. Do you not know your own guests?"

Mick looked around, breathing in the essence of the evening. He saw the two children skip by, no longer frightened and shy but lively and happy, wearing outfits matching Llewellyn's, with little wreaths of oak ivy in their hair.

149

"Oh, yes, I recognize them now. Such wise and noble folk, gathering to celebrate my wedding to the fairest and wisest beauty who ever walked the land."

Llewellyn stepped closer, and Mick reached up to touch one cold, perfect white cheek. "And did you bring anything for me?" asked Llewellyn.

Mick laughed. "Beautiful cloth, and the finest lace, the best I could find."

"Then come in," said Llewellyn softly, "for you have been gone long, and the forest grows dark and cold."

Chapter 11: A Birthday for Vice

Notes: I always found it interesting that, of all the characters in Lord of the Rings that my friend Master Erestor could have named herself after, she chose Lord Elrond's chief advisor. She's certainly given me some very good advice over the years, and it has always proved uncannily accurate. This year, she advised me to spend October the second doing something to make me smile, something that would have made Shane smile, something to turn the day to something positive…

For those of you who do not know, October the second, 1997, is the day my best friend Shane killed herself. Here she is at a party I was throwing.

The ferret's name is Vice, named after this bloke:

This would be Vice the character, not Vice the ferret. This is a rough sketch of him drawn on lined notepaper by Shane. It's the only picture I have of him, other than the one below of him and Cage with the car…

Except you can't really see his face. This is fairly typical for both of them, lost and alone with a broken-down, time-travelling car trapped on an alien planet. I'd like to point out the medium used for this picture is not airbrush; it is felt pen and chalk.

Before Shane died, I had a massive plot bunny that involved a collection of characters she and I jointly created, Vice and Cage included. We both played with them. Some were definitely hers and some were definitely mine, but she gave me her consent to run the little buggers in a novel I was planning. To make a long story short, she died, the bunny went in the hutch, the characters were locked away into cardboard boxes, and life, eventually, went on. I never thought I would touch those characters again. But we all know things have a habit of changing. It's been ten years, and I'm feeling like it's time for the wind to change.

Bless her heart, Master Erestor said (and I'm paraphrasing here): "Do something positive with the day. Something to make you smile."

And I don't know why, but the first thing I thought was, "I should go dig out Vice and Cage and cut them loose." And I swear to whatever god you hold dear, when I opened the folder, Vice and Cage were standing there grinning. Like they knew I'd be back. Gotta admit, it was good to see them. I let them loose briefly in a cheer-up crack!fic for Maldy, just to see if I remembered their paces. No surprise at all that it all came back to me. And… yeah. It felt good.

Made me smile. It felt like I found a piece of myself that had got stuck down between the couch cushions. Frankly, I haven't felt this good in, oh, say, bit over ten years. Not sure when or if I will ever get back to the novel I started with this group, but to handle these guys after so damned long is a real hoot. So I'm doing something positive. Something to make me smile. I'm writing the first honest-to-golly FP story (FP? Wassat?) in ten years.

And there is absolutely only one person to whom I could dedicate this fic. And that is Erestor.

You, my friend, make the world a better place, and me a better person. Enjoy.

* * *

Probably most people know that living in a culvert is cold and wet. I mean, come on. It's a culvert. It's a ditch in the ground where water goes. Okay, it's a pretty nice culvert, but come on, people, it's a culvert.

Well, why do I live in a culvert, you ask? Very good question. Let me answer that in one word: Stacey.

Stacey is why we live in the culvert. Stacey is actually why we do a lot of things around here. Don't ask me where here is. I don't know. I think it used to be London, but I can't swear to it. I can't even swear to being in England. All I know is my boyfriend has an accent that makes him sound like George Harrison when he talks, and I don't care what he says so long as he keeps talking. Preferably while he's got me bent over something. We tried to figure out once if we were in England. We took an old tour book and went around looking for landmarks. All we found was rubble and death. Sometimes bodies. Sometimes kids. The kids we bring home to the culvert. The ones with no parents, that is. I mean, we don't just round up stray kids and take them. We make sure nobody owns them first.

Okay, that came out wrong.

Cage bitches, but he loves them.

Kari is looking over my shoulder and telling me to pick a topic and stay with it. Easy for him to say; he doesn't have to live in this brain. I like Kari. He's honest-to-God-fucking royalty. For real. He's got his pedigree posted on the wall of the warehouse he lives in where he and his boyfriend Brent look after another cache of orphans.

He's got more royals in him than a high-class whore house on a Saturday night. I was looking at it one day.

"You're a fucking Duke!" I said.

"Fat lot of good it does me."

You gotta hear the man talk. Like he's got a mouthful of warm caramel. He's like five-foot-nothing, and he can still look down on you. He can also kick your ass. I should know. He's kicked mine. Him and his other little blue-blood buddy Maxwell. Except Maxwell ain't little.

He's about six-three.

Pick a topic, Vice.

I'm picking a fucking topic already. Just give me a minute here to get shit sorted. There, he left to make tea. That just leaves me and Madman. We call him Madman because he's probably the calmest and most level person I ever met. Actually, his name's Gregory, but nobody calls him that. We all got nicknames. He's Madman because he's not a madman. I'm Vice 'cause Cage says I'm a hard habit to break. Cage is Cage because he ought to be in one. Kari is… Kari.

Okay, so we don't all got nicknames. I used to be 'Yankee' because I think I'm from America. I seem to recall being from Kentucky. Kentucky was a state, right? It's hard to tell. Places just don't exist anymore. I hid on a ship when I was eight and ended up here, thinking it had to be better than where I was from. It wasn't. First person I met was Cage, and he beat the hell out of me. Funny way to start a romance. I have no idea where here is. Other than the culvert.

Okay, good, I finally got to where I started. Kari's applauding.

Asshole.

It's a concrete underground culvert, but I think somebody built it with the idea that, in times of war, people could hide in here. The grates in the streets overhead work, and there's this deep trench through the floor for water to run through, but if you are on the street, you can't see in. You can't really hear anything either. And there are these wide areas where the water doesn't go unless it's a real serious downpour.

Cage and I spent weeks hunting down things in the rubble to make a home. We lucked out and found one of those department stores, and it was mostly intact. Toys, clothes, beds, kitchenware, glasses, kerosene lamps, story books… everything that a couple of queer street-rats need to raise eleven orphans found over a period of two years. Everything but a bed for me and Cage. I'd like a bed. But with eleven kids to look after, everything for us adults is pretty much superfluous.

Hah! Bet you didn't think I knew that word.

We painted their… what would ya call it? Room? Not really a room. Well, whatever it is, we painted it. Five times we painted it. Cage wanted it green. I wanted it lavender. Then Maxwell painted it orange. (We have since learned Maxwell is colour-blind like nobody's business and sees in three shades – black, white, and grey) Madman did it white, and, finally, Kari came over and did it in shades of blue with little stars near the top and grass for the bottom. There were trees and unicorns and Elves. It's so beautiful, I cried. Had a hard time stopping crying, in fact. Cage was kinda worried about me, but I got over it. I guess.

It's a pretty nice place to keep eleven kids who can't go outside. And they don't ask. Like I said, Stacey is the reason we do a lot of things around here. You don't even have to tell people who Stacey is. They know. We know, they know, the kids who have lost parents and siblings to this garbage-heap hyena sure as hell know. We even rewrote that old tune "The Quarter Master's Store" to fit him.

"I have no eyes, I cannot see.
I had a run-in with Stacey…"

That's how we know if it was Stacey who killed someone. The eyes are gone. He's got this whole area pretty much forced underground. Me and Cage had to put up steel doors to keep him out. We don't make much noise after nightfall. I don't think he knows we're down here.

God, I hope he doesn't know we're down here.

We'd like to do something about ol' Stacey. We really would. First, we have to find the sack of crap. So we cooked up a plan. We're gonna go catch Stacey's little boyfriend, Candy Darling. Do not let the name fool you. Just don't. The precious little dear will cut you from butt to breakfast, and he's fast. Small, fast, and pretty. That's Candy. I don't think Candy much likes Stacey either, but he stays with him. He likes breathing like the rest of us. It ain't a good idea to piss off Stacey.

Kari says 'ain't' is not a word. I'll probably come back from taking a leak and find out he's edited this. Him or Madman. Cage says I can be as unliterate as I want, but I think that's just 'cause he's sweet on me.

Who the hell looks at a brand new baby boy and names it Stacey?

Jesus, no wonder the guy's psycho.

It's raining. It's cold. My hip hurts. Wish we had a bed to sleep on. We almost had one. We found a ruined store that sold beds. There was this one there I really liked. It was called a sleigh bed, and it was made out of oak. We were going to go back for it when we had Madman to help us carry it, but the building fell over before we came back. I found it after the collapse, but it was all smashed to crap. That was another time I cried. Cage fucking hates it when I cry because I have a really hard time stopping. Kari says it's because I don't let my emotions out. I think it's because, sometimes, I just can't take one more piece of bad news.

Anyway, I have a pile of sleeping bags, and I have Cage. I'd like a bed like what Tracey and Vance have. That's Tracey, not Stacey. They're different people. Even if at times it's hard to tell the two apart 'cause Tracey can be a massive dick. Tracey and Vance live in an old warehouse, too, like

Kari, but it's just the two of them. They have the bed mounted on some sort of rack so when you pull a chain, it rises up to the rafters of the warehouse. They have some kind of rail so you can't fall off, but it would still scare the shit out of me. But it's safe. Once they're up there, you have no idea there's a couple people in the warehouse. And Vance can shoot the left nut off a horsefly, so if you break in and start trashing the place, you're in a world of hurt.

I think Tracey made the bed. Seems like the sort of thing he would do. He's a freak, and he ain't pretty, let me tell you. He's missing an eye. He wears this patch over the empty socket, and you know what, he keeps his fucking chewing gum in there. Cherry Chiclets. I don't even know where the hell he gets them, but that's where he keeps them. Vance loves Tracey. I don't know why. Tracey is a certifiable asshole. But Vance is in love with him. Tracey says he's not gay, but, come on, ya don't spend three years sleeping in bed with another guy if you don't have some feelings for him. I know they're not having sex. Vance tells me. Tracey's probably hung like a gerbil and afraid if Vance sees that, he will fall out of that bed laughing.

Is just everybody in this area weird, or are all people weird and I never noticed?

* * *

Vice put the pen down and looked up at the concrete ceiling of the culvert, listening to the rain, sensing the impending darkness, thinking he may have heard something other than the downpour. Cotton, the eldest of the children they were looking after, raised his head also, listening.

"Bedtime, I guess," Cotton said. "Time for the Boogeyman to be out."

160

Vice listened carefully but heard nothing other than rain. He turned down the lamp and rose to his feet, distrusting the quiet.

"Get in your room, Cotton. I'll bring dinner."

"Can Madman read us a story?" Cotton waited as Vice listened.

"Yeah, okay," he finally said.

Madman rose to his full six feet, eight inches in height and picked Cotton up, the assault weapon across his back creaking in its harness. Cotton was thirteen and a bit big for being carried around, but he liked it, even if he was now too old and too cool to admit it.

There was a sense of unease in the culvert, like wild animals smelling a predator. Kari rose from his seat and listened as well, his long, curling honey-blonde hair tied back with a bright scrap of blue and red fabric. They stood, frozen in place, and finally heard what they were waiting for: the sudden violent sound of someone immensely powerful ripping at the grate above. No one moved or spoke. Eventually, the noise stopped, and the person left.

"You think he knows we're down here?" asked Vice, his voice a whisper. "He's never been this deep into our territory before."

Kari shook his head. "I very much doubt it. Had he known we were here, he would not have stopped after only a few minutes. He's testing the area, listening for the sound of panic. Speaking of panic, I have a lover and five children at home."

"Go down through the culvert and bring them here," said Vice. "The big drain leads to your warehouse."

Kari left, returning less than an hour later with five small children and his lover. Brent was eleven years younger than Kari, with hair that had turned prematurely grey years ago. He looked haggard and exhausted as he staggered into the sitting area. He had been struggling with pneumonia the past few weeks, and though he was slowly recovering, he was still quite weak. He seated himself in a chair, coughing.

"We have to get rid of him," said Brent. "He's got to go. He knows there are people in this area, and he won't stop hunting until he gets each and every damned one of us."

"Yes, well, it is far easier to *say* 'bell the cat' than it is to actually do so," said Kari.

"If we caught Candy, we would have Stacey right where we want him," said Madman, having returned from reading Cotton and the other children their story.

Vice shoved his pale blonde hair out of his face with one hand. "Yeah, well, catching Candy is not going to be a walk in the park. And what makes you think Stacey cares what happens to Candy anyway? He beats the hell out of him. Pretty sure he tortures him."

"Yeah, but Candy belongs to him," said Madman. "It's not about love with this guy. It's about property rights and control. If we take something of his, he'll combust. He will tear this entire place apart looking for it. If we catch Candy, we have Stacey right where we want him. We can lead him into any trap we want."

"It would be nice to not have to dart like rats to a pipe every evening," said Kari.

They paused, listening, hearing footsteps. But this time, the faint sounds they heard turned out to be Cage returning, a duffle bag across his back and a large box in his arms.

"Jackpot," he said, grinning, and set the box down. "I don't know what the hell these are, but there's enough food here to keep us going for a few months. We can go back in the morning and get more. There's a ton of this shit." Cage set down the duffle bag, then grabbed Vice, pushing him down onto the table and kissing him hard. Kari, Madman and Brent watched.

"Rather like watching bulls mate, isn't it?" said Kari as Cage's broad, powerful body pinned Vice's slimmer one to the table.

"And do you spend a lot of time watching bulls mate?" asked Madman.

"Oh, yes. Every other Thursday, in fact."

Cage ran his large hand over Vice's body, kissing him hard. Brent reached into the box and pulled out a foil-wrapped packet, opening it. His eyes lit up.

"Bloody hell, look at this! Matches, meat, *coffee*! Toilet paper. God, I haven't seen toilet paper in so long, I think I'll have an orgasm."

"And now you have something with which to wipe it up," said Kari. Brent grinned and kissed him.

Cage raised his head. "Found a container truck full of those. All the other trucks had been smashed open and raided, so I guess no one thought there was anything left. I even brought some over to Vance and Tracey." He returned his gaze to Vice. "Hello, lovely." He resumed kissing him passionately.

"Oh, good, now Tracey has something else to stick in his socket," said Madman. "Look, will you two kindly stop fornicating all over the rations?"

"Did you find me a bed?" asked Vice.

Cage kissed his nose. "Sorry. I looked. Your hip bothering you?"

"Nah, I'm fine. I got you."

Kari, Brent, and Madman all made suitable gagging and barfing sounds.

Cage looked over his shoulder at them. "Why are you assholes in my house?"

"Oh, why does anything happen around here?" sighed Kari as he and Brent opened a few of the packages to make coffee.

"Stacey? Here?"

"Yeah, we heard him just a short while ago, testing the grates," said Madman.

"Son of a fucking bitch," said Cage. "I'd like to put a bullet in him."

"We've got a plan," said Madman.

"Oh, yeah?"

"Yeah. We're gonna catch Candy and use him as bait."

"Though how we are to accomplish this monumental task, I have not the faintest idea," said Kari.

Cage looked thoughtful. Reaching out, he picked up one of the packaged meals, looking at it with a thoughtful expression. "Believe it or not, I think I do."

* * *

"Brilliant," said Tracey. "You're all a pack of assholes." He shoved his greying hair back with one scarred hand.

"I don't see you coming up with anything better," said Kari.

Tracey stared at the small pile of rations being heaped in a "careless" manner on a box at the far side of a dead-end alley by Madman. He finished laying the bait and returned to the area where his friends were hiding.

"How stupid do you think the man is?" said Tracey. "He's gonna know it's a trap!"

"He comes down this way almost nightly," said Cage. "I know he does because people in the area see him."

"Stacey would crack his skull if he knew Candy had a routine," said Vice.

Cage nodded. "Yeah, he would. But this alley is a stashing site for some of the people who live around here. Candy knows that. He comes here to raid supplies."

"Seems like a daft place to hide your food supply," said Brent.

"Not that daft," said Madman. "The old stonework keeps it cool so it lasts longer, and the dead-end makes it easier to guard. You can't see them, but there are three people with rifles on the roof over there.

165

I had to pay them off with a crate of Cage's rations to let us set up this little trap."

"Well, if Candy comes down here to raid, why don't they shoot him?" asked Tracey. Then he realized. "Because the demented gorilla he belongs to would come kill them all. Right. Forget I asked."

"Speaking of Candy," said Brent, "there he is."

Five heads dropped behind a barrier of old crates and discarded furniture, peeking between cracks and crevices to watch the small, solitary form walk down the alley. He was white, almost luminously so. White skin, white hair, large soft blue eyes set in a delicate, heart-shaped face. He was small, his long white hair falling loose over his shoulders and down his back to his hips. He looked fragile and helpless and oh-so-very pitifully alone. The five guys behind the crates were not buying it for a moment. Cage still remembered having to pick the tip of a knife out of his rib with a pair of tweezers from his last encounter with the little darling.

Candy walked into the alley blithely, far too accustomed to being unchallenged on these streets. But when he spied the packaged food, he stopped dead and looked around, almost instinctively realizing something was wrong. The people who stored their food here did not leave it lying around in plain site for any thief and rat to find.

Cautiously he began backing out of the alley, one small hand reaching for the large bowie knife on his belt.

The five leapt out, screaming, the idea being to overwhelm the small man with noise and surprise. The

166

result, however, was to send Candy into utter panic, and he turned into a whirling ball of death. His fourteen-inch bowie knife stabbed into Madman's thigh as he kicked out with one booted foot, catching Cage neatly in the groin. He pulled his knife out of Madman's leg and spun, slashing Tracey across the face, and then was gone, tearing into the darkness, his white hair flying behind him.

"You and your brilliant fucking plans," said Cage, lying on his side, curled up in a foetal position, holding his swelling testicles.

"Shut up," said Madman, ripping up his shirt to tie around the gaping wound in his leg. "Tracey? How you doing over there?"

"Little fucker almost took out the *other* eye!"

Vice and Kari tore after the tiny streak of white that was Candy. He was astonishingly quick and unpredictable in his movements. He would feint left and then dart right, head down alleys then double back, leap over fences, climb walls and into windows. There was nowhere he would not go, and because he was so little, he could fit into places Vice simply couldn't and into a few spots too small for even Kari to go. Still, they kept after him, chasing their only chance of ridding themselves of the local nightmare.

"We're losing him," said Vice.

"Bloody hell we are!" said Kari. "Go left!"

Vice tore down the alley Kari indicated, while Kari himself kept after Candy. Vice emerged right before the tiny man, who stopped dead. Candy turned, spying Kari coming up fast behind him.

"It's okay," said Vice, "we're not going to hurt you. We just... Crap! Little *fucker*!"

Candy went sideways, leaping up to catch hold of the top of an eight-foot-high board fence. He was over it in a second and landed on the other side with a screech of indignity. There came the noise of a brief struggle. Then, a few moments later, a familiar face peered over the fence, black hair askew, nose streaming blood.

"Caught the little shit."

"Vance?" said Vice. "Where the hell did you come from?"

"I've been following the chase from the rooftops. I figured he would head here. There are large pipes leading into the old sewers and holes in the brickwork. He would have lost you guys in a second. So I took a chance this is where he would go and laid in wait."

There was muffled screeching, screaming, and swearing. Vice walked over to the fence, panting and shaky from the long chase. He peered through the wooden slats and watched as Vance dropped down from the pile of debris he had been standing on to look over the fence. He picked up something thrashing and snarling that was wrapped in an area rug.

"He's kinda mad," said Vance.

Vice cocked an eyebrow. "I would be, too, if I was tied up in a mouldy rug that smelled like cat piss."

"It's his own tough luck for shagging the enemy. Come on, let's get out of here before the little darling's boyfriend shows up and takes a flying leap at a random orifice, then sucks our eyes out of our skulls for dessert."

Candy snarled a truly impressive array of threats, insults, and profanity, the blade of his knife punching through the rank carpet as he tried to cut his way out. Vance dropped the rug and kicked it.

"Settle down in there, or you'll get a fresh coat of piss! And it won't be cat!"

The knife withdrew. But the snarling, swearing, and threats continued unabated. Kari smiled, reaching up fix the scrap of cloth holding back his long hair.

"Well, we have the beauty for the bait. Let us see now if our offering lures the beast."

* * *

I'm back. Boy, I hurt. Running all over the place after Candy just about wrecked me. My hip feels like it's on fire. Not looking forward to lying on concrete tonight. And it's October, too. I know the kids get cold at night, but at least they're off the floor and have blankets. Tonight, we pushed four of the beds together and threw two of our sleeping bags over top of their blankets. So with body heat and more covers, there haven't been any complaints of not being able to sleep because of the cold. It means less insulation between me and the concrete, but what can ya do? Can't leave the little shits to freeze. Kari brought over a real prize – a goose down comforter, king-sized, of course. Have no idea where he got it. That went to the kids, too. He and Brent are huddled together in the kids' room. We're all on edge. Come morning, when Candy don't come home, Stacey is gonna shit land mines.

Sorry, I just had to envision that for a second.

169

Madman's gone. I have no idea where he goes. He takes off for days at a time and comes back like nothing ever happened. I think he's got a little honey stashed somewhere, but I don't know anything about it. I'm pretty sure he went to his girlfriend/boyfriend/favourite drinking buddy's house to rest that leg wound. That's the sort of shit Madman would do. I know he's got an old wreck of a Jeep, but I wouldn't want to drive on that leg. Hope he's okay.

Candy's asleep. I mean dead asleep. Exhausted. Don't think he's too busted up about being our captive. He wolfed down three of those packaged things Cage found, hardly even bothered unwrapping them. Then he curled up like an animal and, bam, out cold. He's pencil thin, and his back, chest, and arms are so heavily scarred, he doesn't look real. It's bad enough knowing Stacey is prowling the streets. I can't imagine living with that monster.

Gonna go to bed now. Oops. Maybe not. Eyeballs lookin' at me.

* * *

Vice put down his pen and looked at the little girl peeking back at him from over the edge of the old battered table he and Cage had dragged down into the culvert ages ago. She was very small, only about four years old. Vice had no idea how old the child was. Birthdays were a forgotten art. Her long, thick, brown hair hung loose and messy around her little face, making her green eyes look enormous.

"Katie, why are you up?" asked Vice.

"Brent's making noises."

"What kind of noises."

She imitated them, a sort of snorting, wheezing noise. "Like that. I can't sleep."

"Well, go kick him in the butt."

"Uh-uh! Last time I did that, he said if I did it again, he'd spank me so hard, my ass would fall off."

Kari walked into the area, yawning, wearing a pair of jeans and Brent's old green army sweater. His feet were bare despite the cold. "Katie do not swear, you're only little."

"Mommy and Daddy do."

Kari paused and looked at the little girl. "I beg your pardon? Mommy and Daddy?"

"Yeah!" Katie looked at Vice. "Are you Mommy or Daddy?"

"I'm your mommy. Unless you've been bad, then Cage is your mommy."

"Oh." She helped herself to some of Vice's hot chocolate, then belched loudly.

Kari was appalled. "Katie what do you say after you burp?"

The child thought. "Well, Cage says 'thank God it didn't come out the other way, or I would have shit myself.'"

Vice burst out laughing as Kari stared in horror.

"Please tell me you know better than that."

Vice was still giggling. "Katie, what do you say after you burp?"

The child thought for a moment. "Thank you?"

Vice howled with amusement. Kari just shook his head.

"There ought to be organizations in place to prevent people like you from raising children."

"Look, I fell in love with another man. What more do you want me to do?" Vice accepted his chocolate back from Katie. "I keep finding random kids all over the city."

"I'm not random!" said Katie hotly. "I take baths!"

Vice snorted hot chocolate, his hand over his mouth, trying to prevent the liquid from shooting all over. His mirth, however, died an abrupt and icy death as he heard a loud voice, uncomfortably close, bellowing a name.

"*Candy!*"

Katie's eyes grew large, and she uttered a small cry of fright. "It's the boogeyman!"

Kari scooped her up and took her back to the room she shared with the other children. Vice doused the light and stood in the blackness of the culvert, listening to Stacey bawl to the heavens above like some wounded beast.

"*Candy!*"

Vice heard a brief struggle in the next room and Cage's voice.

"Come on, time to earn your keep."

Vice stepped out of the chamber and into the trench through which the water ran. Currently, there was a steady stream flowing because of the rain. He watched as Cage wrestled Candy out of the small chamber where they had been keeping him, having to fight to keep the much smaller man under control. Candy was struggling for all he was worth, biting like a wild animal.

"Cage what are you doing?" asked Vice.

Cage was flustered and angry, his dark hair askew. "This is what we caught the little shit for, isn't it? Bait?"

"We don't need him for bait anymore. The bastard is right outside!"

"Yeah, well, maybe I'm just feeling mean," said Cage.

Kari returned from the children's room. "Cage, I understand your anger, but killing Candy won't fix our problem, and it certainly won't harm Stacy any. He'll just go track down some other victim."

Slowly, reluctantly, Cage released the smaller man. Vice understood his rage, how very badly he wanted to hurt Stacey, even at the expense of another's life. They had all lived under the shadow of this monster a long time. But killing Candy wouldn't mend a damned thing. Kari reached a hand out to Candy, who went to him, slowly, nervously, as if wondering whether or not Kari would finish the job Cage had begun.

"We have him where we want him," said Kari. "There is no need to kill anyone because you are angry."

"*Angry*?" said Cage. "Oh, I am well beyond angry. There is no name for what I feel. Not anger, not hate, not rage… there are no words for what I feel. Do you know how many friends I have lost to that monster? Friends, acquaintances, kids that Vice and I were raising? Doesn't make any difference that I wasn't their father, those were *my* kids!"

"Do you know what it's like to *live* with that animal?" shot Candy, his voice filled with an equal amount of grief and hate. "I'm not your enemy."

"Well, we have to come up with a plan of attack," said Vice. "He's right outside, and we have no idea where Madman is, and the three of us…"

"Four," said Candy. "Give me my knife. I can fight."

"Won't get no argument from me," said Cage. "You killed my sex life for the next three weeks, that's for sure."

"Ergo, you have also killed Vice's," said Kari.

Vice thought about that for a moment. "Let's feed the little bleached shit to his boyfriend."

"Bleached?" squawked Candy, indignant.

"Can Brent fight?" asked Cage.

Kari shook his head. "No, he can barely breathe. We shall have to make do with…"

The scream carried through the culvert, wild and full of terror, the shriek of a child in desperate circumstances. The discussion ended, and all four bolted in the direction of the sound. They tore out of the entrance of the culvert like a pack of wolves, Vice hitting the huge man first, launching himself at him like a starving animal, forcing him to drop Cotton. Cage grabbed the boy and dragged him away from the fight, looking him over. The child was cut and battered, but he could have been much worse.

"Back inside," was all Cage said. The boy ran for the culvert, vanishing into the depths.

The fight was brutal and quick. There was no artful choreography, no witty banter, no conveniently placed weapons. It was fast and dirty and bloody, the wolf pack defending the den from a primordial beast that lived only to kill and to feed on still-breathing flesh. Candy landed on Stacey's back like a Valkyrie, raising the blade of his knife over his head and slamming it into the huge back with all his might. The pain only enraged the enormous man they did battle with, and he grabbed Vice around the throat and threw him as if he were a sack of potatoes. Vice hit a wall of crumbling brick and bounced off, dropping to the cobblestone street and lying motionless. The last thing he heard before all went dark was the rain and the sound of Cage screaming his name.

* * *

Vice managed to open one eye. The other was not working. He had no idea if that meant it was gone or not. He looked around and managed a smile, feeling the stitches in his lip pull as he saw the bruised and haggard form of Cage sitting beside him on the floor.

"Hey," said Vice.

"Hi," said Cage. "You had us worried."

"Mph. I'm fine. How come I can only see out of my left eye?"

"Because your right eye was bandaged shut after Madman stuffed it back into the socket." Cage gently stroked Vice's pale blonde hair. "Thought you were dead."

"What? And leave you alone to find somebody else? Not a chance. How's Cotton?"

Cage growled. "Little bugger will be just fine. We're just waiting for him to heal so I can beat the stupid out of him."

175

"Cage..."

"He's fine, Vice, he's fine. Little shaken up, few bruises and cuts, but he's fine. Stacey didn't get a chance to do any serious damage."

"What was the kid doing out there?"

"Oh, he had some brilliant thirteen-year-old-boy idea that he could get Stacey in the head with his sling shot, be a big hero, save us all. Be a long time 'fore he tries that again."

"Did we get him?"

Cage toyed gently with Vice's bloody hair. "No," he finally said. "But we put the run to him. Kari and I hunted him all the way down to the old dock 'fore we lost him. Candy said that's one of his haunts, so we torched the place. You can still see the light in the distance." He kissed Vice softly. "He knows we're not going to be his meat anymore. Candy's staying. He's showing us where the bastard lives. We'll get him. Don't you worry. Want me to get you anything?"

Vice closed his eyes. "Yeah, a bed."

"I'll see if we have one in any of those little packets."

"Just lie beside me. Please. I feel so awful."

Cage did, settling on the thin, inadequate mat covering the concrete floor. "Just rest, babe. I'm here."

* * *

Spring haz sprung, the grass has riz, I wonder where da bodies is.

I have no idea where I heard that, but I still think it once in a while. I thunk of it a lot more when I was younger. Thunk? Kari says 'thought,' and 'thunk' is not a word. It's a sound effect. He also says I'm the blonde responsible for the

176

bad reputation bestowed upon all blondes. I told him it wasn't me that one time who thought it was a good idea to light a match to check where the smell of gas was coming from.

Good news is no one has seen Stacey since we kicked his ass and burned a bunch of his hide-outs. He's in his own little corner of hell, wherever that is. It's not here, and that's all I care about. Cage can take the kids out. They go to what used to be a park. There are trees there. Cherry, apple, pear. There's a house back there, too. Has fireplaces and windows. Cage and Madman and Kari have been fixing it up so we can go live there. I can't do much. I never really recovered from the fight. Kari says he thinks it was the cold. He thinks I might have aurther-itis, whatever that is. I can't even spell it.

Kari says it's arthritis. Who cares? It hurts. Just want to be warm. That's all. Just want to be warm. Plants are starting to bud and bloom, but it's still so damned cold.

Katie read a story about birthdays, and now she wants one. She has decided she's going to be six. She could be, I guess. We told her that she could have a birthday when we move into the house. Cage found a calendar in the house. We figure it's about February, so that's where we're starting it at. We can just keep using it, I guess. Katie is all excited. We have eleven kids, so everyone gets their own month, and there's one month leftover for me and Cage to share.

I'd share a month with Cage, all right. I'd share a lifetime with him.

Funny how no one asked what I'd like for my birthday. I think they all probably know.

* * *

Vice looked up as Cage came in, dirty and grinning. He walked over to Vice and kissed him.

"Come along, house is ready, and we're all moved in. Grab your diary."

Vice scooped up the collection of pages with their inky scrawls and slowly, painfully stood up. Cage put an arm around him and helped him out of the room.

"It's going to be hard leaving here," said Vice.

"Thought you hated this place."

"I do. It's cold and damp, but we've lived here a long time. I'll miss it."

"No, you won't. Wait until you see the new house. We have a fireplace in our room. You can be warm tonight. And there's a wood stove and a bathtub. Hot baths for everybody."

Vice closed his eyes in anticipation. "That sounds so good."

"Come along. I got you."

It was not a long walk, but it was hellishly difficult for Vice. He could not go far before having to rest, but he determinedly kept on, finally reaching the house. It was a large house, well-built, solid, and still beautiful despite the years of neglect. It had been cleaned, broken windows replaced with glass scavenged from other areas, the front and back doors replaced with solid wooden ones. The furniture had been moved in, the fireplace was lit, and the entire house was filled with blessed warmth. It was so good to finally at long last feel the soft kiss of heat on his chilled bones that Vice's eyes filled with tears.

"Here, now, don't start that," said Cage. "*Please* don't start. Dammit, Vice, I can't deal with it when you cry like that!"

"I'm sorry. I really am. I just… feel so much better."

"Yeah, well, save it. I got you something special for your birthday."

Vice wiped at his eyes impatiently, looking puzzled. "My what?"

"Your birthday! It's today! Had a chat with Katie, and she agreed to swap months. So now we're February, and she's March."

"Oh. Okay. Why?"

Cage picked Vice up, not an easy task. Vice may have been slimmer than Cage, but he was still tall and well-muscled. Lifting him was almost more than Cage could manage. Carrying Vice up two flights of steps nearly killed him.

"Cage? You can put me down."

Cage staggered and wheezed. "Almost there."

"Well, don't drop me."

"I'm not going to drop you, just quit your bitching."

Cage carried Vice to the uppermost floor, then gently set him on his feet, panting and gasping.

"Are you going to die?" asked Vice.

Cage shook his head, catching his breath. "Not at the moment. Come on."

They walked down the hall to the room at the end of the short passage. The rotting carpets had been torn out, revealing somewhat damaged but still attractive hardwood floors. Cage reached out to turn the handle on the door at the end of the hall. It opened, and Vice uttered a slow gasp of disbelief as he spied what lay within the chamber. It was an old-fashioned sleigh-style bed, piled with quilts and pillows, topped by a red down comforter printed with a soft grey design. The headboard and footboard were carved of oak, and the mattress was easily large enough for both of them and most of the kids. Vice burst into tears, and Cage rolled his eyes.

"It's supposed to make you *happy*, ya naff bastard!"

Vice punched him in the shoulder, then cried harder. "I *am* happy!"

"Well, if you're going to cry all over it, then you can't sleep on it!"

Vice collapsed against Cage, holding him tightly as he wept against his neck. Cage gently stroked his hands over Vice's back, comforting him.

"So does this mean you like it?"

Vice sniffed, then nodded, laughing through his tears. "I love it. And I love you. Thank you."

Cage smiled. "Happy birthday, Vice," he said and kissed him.

Chapter 12: The Thunder-Horse

He was Nathan's horse. He was from the moment they saw each other. He was a huge black Friesian stallion, with an arched neck and massive hairy hooves, fighting his lead and snorting as he was taken out of the trailer and onto the set where they were shooting the video. The first thing the brute did was rear up and bellow his intense dislike of the mortals he was forced to suffer, iron-shod hooves scraping the air. Andrew was not impressed.

"We requested a horse for a shoot, and you bring us a nightmare?"

"He'll settle down," said the handler.

Andrew watched the aggressive, unhappy animal and made a mental note to not use these animal-handlers again. Granted, as the personal assistant of one of the biggest, both literally and figuratively, rock stars on the planet, it was *not* his job to do things like acquire animals for video shoots, but Nathan Maynard trusted few people and liked even fewer. So it fell to Andrew to get the horse for the video shoot, and what they had ended up with was not a horse but a nightmare. Terrific. Well, there went his Christmas bonus.

Andrew could not help but notice the other three members of the band were standing well away from glorious and highly pissed-off animal. He watched as Nathan approached the unhappy horse, beer in hand, wincing as he pictured one of the massive hooves smashing Nathan's skull like an egg.

Nathan walked up to the huge, hairy beast, its long black mane hanging over its face, froth dripping from its jaws as though it was rabid. Man and horse regarded each other.

"Let's just get this shit over with," Nathan said.

The horse stole his can of beer and downed it, then spat the empty at the handler. It was love at first sight.

The song was one of those old-style power ballads, well-suited to a video full of cowboy and Wild West imagery, despite the fact that their lead guitar player, Adalwolf, was German and barely spoke a word of English. But he was tall and spectacular and looked absolutely fantastic dressed up like a cowboy, his long reddish-blonde hair blowing in the dry dusty wind. At least he did until he had a bizarrely phobic reaction to a passing tumbleweed and went tearing off the set as if he was being chased by three dragons and a flaming troll. The drummer and bass player were no help; Daryl and Bill just laughed.

Still, Adalwolf's newly-discovered terror of free-roaming bushes was hardly the main difficulty of the video shoot. They had to teach Nathan to ride, and the horse he had to ride was extremely large and had already let it be known he didn't like people. But that was fine with Nathan; he didn't like people either. It was Andrew's job to deal with people and to let Nathan get on with the business of making music.

Andrew actually did far more than tend to the pointless necessities that went with his boss being a major rock star. It was his job to protect Nathan and keep a buffer between him and other human beings.

Being talented and charismatic didn't make him good with other people. Nathan didn't like people and had no reason to like them. He wasn't smart, although he wasn't too stupid to know he was frequently mocked for being a little slow.

As a small child, his parents had been in the habit of forcing him to sleep in the car in the closed garage so they couldn't hear his screams for food and comfort in the middle of the night. There had been other forms of abuse as well, and the pain and terror inflicted on little Nathan had not been forgotten when one day little Nathan became big Nathan – big as in six-foot-nine, three hundred and twenty pounds, and toned and powerful from years of working his rage out in the boxing ring. Nathan's father Phil had shown up exactly once to try and mooch off his famous son. He spent three months in the hospital as a result.

Nathan rarely smiled, and despite being rich and famous and talented as both a fighter and a singer, he didn't enjoy life so much as endure it. The only people he seemed to actually like were his bandmates, and even they were kept at a certain distance. But he liked the horse, and the horse liked him. It made Andrew genuinely happy right down to his Gucci dress shoes to see Nathan respond to something living and to have that thing return his interest.

From what Andrew was able to gather speaking to the horse wranglers, the beautiful Friesian stallion had not had a happy childhood either and had suffered being ill and neglected first at a breeding farm more interested in profit than care, and then again at the hands of a rescuer who turned out to be little more than an emotionally disturbed animal hoarder. Eventually, he ended up in the hands of the company that currently owned him, where he remained disgruntled and embittered with the human race.

Small wonder Nathan and the horse were bonding. Still, it was obvious that the two brought out the best in each other, and it wasn't long before Nathan and the great beast were tearing around the Texas scrub like the Lone Ranger and Silver.

"Gonna break his heart when we have to give that horse back," said Daryl, watching Nathan ride by.

Andrew had been thinking the same thing, and while he was all in favour of anything that made Nathan happy, the animal simply did not belong to them. But Nathan seemed to have overlooked that detail. So had the horse, apparently, because the day they came to take him away, the animal fought his handlers every inch of the way, bracing his hooves in the dirt and refusing to move.

Andrew did not believe the animal was mistreated, but he doubted it got much in the way of attention that was not related to work. Still, it made him ill to watch the two men try to fight the mighty equine into his trailer. Then, at one point, the horse reared, trying to pull free, but succeeded only in slipping and falling heavily. Nathan, unable to stand it anymore, walked over to the handlers to take the lead, growling at the smaller man as the horse slowly got to his feet, shaking and a little dazed.

"Fuck off," said Nathan to the handler.

"What do you mean, fuck off?" asked the handler.

"I mean leave my horse alone."

"I think you mean *my* horse!"

"No, I mean I'll mail you a cheque for what he's worth, and you can cash it or shove up your ass or whatever the fuck makes you happy."

The handler stared at Nathan as he turned to the black horse and took off the lead rope and halter, dropping them onto the ground. He reached up and took hold of the pointed ears, bending them gently, pressing his face to the animal's.

"Stupid horse," he said. He then released it, gave it a slap on the shoulder and walked away, the great Friesian following amicably at his side.

"I need a beer," muttered Nathan.

The horse snorted in what sounded like agreement. The handlers simply packed up their gear and left, in no mood to face off with Nathan Maynard. Nathan, it seemed, had just bought a horse.

The creature's name was Lord Willoughby's Shades of Evening, but no one called him that. He was Horse. Andrew had at first worried Nathan would get bored, and the animal would be left to rot in a paddock, but that didn't happen. Even when Nathan had no time for him, *someone* was with Horse. He was never left to wallow in loneliness, neglected and forgotten.

Daryl would go talk to him and braid his shaggy mane, though he never expressed any interest in trying to get on him. Adalwolf would ride Horse occasionally, but normally he would go out and brush him when he was pissed off with life, bitching the whole time in German while Horse munched hay.

Even Bill would go talk to him, occasionally sitting on him backwards. Horse didn't seem to care. He didn't even appear to mind that Bill seemed to have no understanding of the differences between a horse and a dog and endured him with good humour as Bill taught him to speak, shake, and fetch. Bill actually only rode Horse once, and it was a short-lived experience. He had never been on a horse, and he did not know what he was doing. He accidentally pulled too hard on the right rein, and Horse, who had lived most of his life being taught behaviours for movies, assumed that was his cue to fall over, which he did. Bill was flattened under Horse like a bug, and he never got on his back again.

Adalwolf was the one who rode Horse the most. He was red cowboy death on a horse. He had apparently done some riding in his youth with a hunt club, as well as some roping, and he quickly became the terror of every employee on the grounds of the large estate the band collectively owned and inhabited within lasso range. He would come tearing along, reins in one hand, lariat in the other, and, with deftness rare to find in even experienced cattle ropers, snare a gardener or groundskeeper and have him hog-tied in record time.

Soon, the most fearsome sound on the manor grounds was that German accent screaming, "*Yeeeeeaaaaaaaa-HOOOO!*" accompanied by thundering hooves.

Most people bore this without complaint, until the day Adalwolf branded one on the ass. Andrew still recalled that. He had been sitting in his office when the head gardener Taylor came storming in, dirty, dusty, and limping.

He yanked off his hat, brown hair at all angles, face red, and yelled, "I *quit!* I am *out* of here! I was willing to put up with living in a house with a bunch of thirty-year-old juvenile delinquents, but *nobody* said *anything* about having to put up with getting hog-tied and having my *ass* branded!"

"I'm sorry," said Andrew, "you were…?"

"*Branded!*" Taylor turned so Andrew could see his hip. Sure enough, he had been branded. And not a little brand, either. This was a good old-fashioned cowboy brand, meant to be seen and recognized from a distance.

Andrew stared at the brand and was horrified to realize he was starting to laugh.

"Well," he said, clearing his throat, fighting back his hilarity. "I really had thought there was nothing left they could do to surprise me, but… *that* surprises me." He fought back an urge to laugh his head off, though whether it was humour or hysteria he wasn't quite sure. "Well… if you insist on quitting, I'm sure we can come up with adequate compensation for the damages you suffered."

Taylor, now that he had calmed down a little, was starting to grin himself. "No, that's fine, I don't want to quit. But can I *please* be transferred somewhere out of roping range?"

Andrew found the urge to laugh becoming harder to fight. He brought his hand over his mouth, squeezing his eyes shut. Taylor was starting to giggle himself as he continued speaking.

"I mean I'm standing there, minding my own business, and Wild Bill Adalwolf comes hurtling around a corner. The next thing I know, I'm on my face, tied up with my ass in the air, and a man in chaps is coming at me with a big glowing piece of iron. Now that is *not* a comfortable feeling!"

Andrew desperately fought the urge to burst out laughing. He almost had it under control until Taylor added, "All I could think was thank God he didn't have a set of bull castrators..."

Andrew rode Horse a few times himself, though he couldn't help but think the animal had a definite sense of sarcasm. The first time Horse got a look at Andrew in his riding gear, Andrew would have sworn the animal raised an eyebrow and muttered "Oh, puh-leeze!" Horse stood patiently as Andrew got the English-style saddle on him, then when the small man climbed onto his back, Horse turned his head to look at him, as if asking "Are you done yet?"

"Come along," Andrew said.

Horse tilted an ear, then, without any urging from Andrew whatsoever, pranced out of the stall with high, exaggerated steps. Andrew was sure he could hear the horse mentally singing, *"Here we go gathering nuts in May, nuts in May, nuts in May..."* Andrew was willing to let him get away with it, but when Horse turned towards a tree and began picking up speed, Andrew curbed him so sharply that Horse was almost forced onto his ass. Man and animal regarded each other.

"Please don't fuck with me," said Andrew. "I don't like it."

Horse never tried to scrape Andrew off against a tree again.

In many ways, Horse belonged to all of them, but in Horse's mind, he belonged to Nathan. The two would go for long walks together, Horse following along at his side, no halter, no lead, just walking of his own accord. Occasionally, Nathan would go to the stall, and the two would lounge together, Horse lying in the hay, Nathan leaning against his powerful back. They would share a six pack, Horse spitting the empties across the room. Sometimes, Nathan rode him, but when he did, he never used a bridle or saddle. He would climb onto the broad back, tangle his hands into the long black mane, and off they would go, often for hours. These were the times Andrew resented the most, chastising himself for being jealous of an animal.

Andrew had been with Nathan a few times, and while Nathan was happy to share his body, he was far more hesitant about sharing his emotions. It was a problem he didn't seem to have with Horse, and Andrew couldn't help but resent it. Andrew had considered withdrawing from the relationship, telling himself that occasional sex with a man who did not want to have him spend the night in his bed wasn't worth his time. But Andrew couldn't seem to make himself turn Nathan away the times when he did come to him.

It was not a satisfying arrangement, but Andrew endured it, hoping some day it would turn into more. However, as the months went by, Nathan gave no indication of wanting to further the relationship. So Andrew stewed in silence and took the bits he was offered, resenting the meagre offerings as well as the animal that seemed to hold far more of Nathan's heart than he ever would.

Andrew still remembered the evening he found himself standing in Horse's stall, watching as Nathan and Horse rode at full speed through the slashing rain of a summer storm, both soaking wet, water streaming down Horse's black coat and Nathan's long hair. They entered the stall, steaming and dripping, and Andrew was dead certain he had never seen anything so damned erotic as Nathan with his shirt and jeans clinging to his large body, his hair plastered to his face and throat, controlling that huge horse with only his thighs and hands.

Andrew didn't even mind waiting while Nathan got Horse cooled and dried and clean, hating himself for being resigned to play second fiddle to an animal and hating himself even more for feeling that rush of joy and want when Nathan finally turned to him, covered in hair, soaking wet and smelling of rain and horse and hay. Maybe a little of something was better than nothing. It didn't seem to matter much once he was naked and on his back with that huge, powerful body on top of him, feeling Nathan thrust deep and hard into him, muttering quiet obscenities into his ear.

Andrew still remembered watching Nathan walk up to Horse after they were done and getting ready to leave. He took the animal's ears in his hands and gently pulled them, pressing his face against Horse's, looking into the dark eyes.

"Stupid horse."

He rose up on his toes to whisper something into a furry ear, then went to get him a snack before bed, having to open a new bag of feed to do so. Andrew finished dressing and stood up. He reached out to pat the powerful neck, and then he and Nathan departed, leaving Horse warm, dry, and content in his large stall, each heading to his own room once more. Stupid horse was right. But the situation was hardly Horse's fault. Still, it made for cold comfort as Andrew went to his room alone, his flesh still smeared with Nathan's semen. He showered, then set the alarm and went to bed, eventually falling asleep.

At 4:37 in the morning, Taylor woke Andrew up.

"It's Horse," was all he said.

"Did you call a vet?" Andrew asked.

The man nodded. "Yeah, that was the first thing I did."

"Do Nathan and the guys know?"

"No."

"Good. Don't tell them. With luck, by the time they wake up, this will have been resolved. No point in upsetting them."

But by the time Bill showed up to give Horse his morning feeding, he was dead.

The band wouldn't let Horse be taken away. Instead, they cut out the floor of his stall and dug a grave themselves, burying Horse in the place where he had lived the last eighteen months of his life. They bolted the lower half of the stall doors closed, but chained the upper doors open. They loaded in hay, filled the manger and water trough, and left a six pack beside his oat bucket. Then they made their way back to their rooms and locked themselves in. After all, it wasn't cool to be seen crying over the family pet.

Andrew dealt with his own grief a little differently. He sent samples of Horse's feed out for analysis, finding the grain was heavily tainted with a number of toxins due to improper storage at the feed plant. Andrew sued them off the face of the earth, venting his rage at the hurt done to his demented little family the only way he knew how. In the end, the plant was little more than an abandoned warehouse, Horse was still dead, and Andrew was left with a sick lump of guilt that he could have harboured such animosity towards something that had brought so much joy into the life of a man who had endured more than his fair share of pain.

It was weeks before there was some semblance of normalcy in the manor. The first sign of life was Bill in the rehearsal space, playing bass by himself. Eventually, as the days passed, he was joined by Adalwolf and Daryl, and the usual nonsense that went with trying to write music.

Nathan had yet to emerge.

Andrew finally went to his room, entering quietly. He spied Nathan leaning against the windowsill, gazing out into the evening at Horse's paddock. Andrew walked up to him, slipping an arm around him.

"Nathan, you can't stay in here forever."

Nathan did not react to his presence at first. Then he said quietly, "It's my fault. I killed Horse."

"No, you didn't. The feed was bad. That was what killed Horse."

"No. I did it."

"Nathan, you did not kill Horse. You loved him."

"I know. And I told him. I whispered it in his ear that night. That's why he died."

Andrew gave him a puzzled look. "I don't understand."

"Oh, come on, Andrew, have you ever noticed that no one around here uses the 'L' word for anything other than beer and cheese? Because everything we love dies." Nathan stared down into the empty paddock. "That's… why… I can't ever tell you. And why I never let you stay the night."

Outside, there was a brief flash of lightning. Eventually, there was thunder. The storm was far away, muted and dull, as everything had been of late. Did Nathan really think everything he loved was going to be taken from him in some brutal way? Is that why Nathan never let him stay the night, never gave him more than the merest hints of affection? It made sense. It was not as if his life had been filled with warmth and affection. Andrew reached out to touch Nathan's hair.

"Can I assume that means you… dislike me a great deal?"

A slight smile crossed Nathan's face. "Yeah. Might even be complete loathing."

Andrew smiled, closing his eyes as Nathan lowered his head so their brows met, feeling a weight lift from his chest, replaced by a joy that made him want to sing. "I was afraid I didn't mean anything to you."

"No. You mean a lot. That's why… I couldn't tell you. I was… well… scared you'd go. Leave. Be killed. Something."

"I would really like to stay the night."

"I can't let you do that."

The lightning flickered again, and Andrew was startled by the brief image of a huge horse in the paddock, mane and tail blowing, gazing back at the window.

"Is that…? I mean…did I just see…?"

"He's out there every night," said Nathan.

The lightning flickered again, but this time, all Andrew saw was empty paddock. He was not a man given to such things as fancying he saw phantom horses, but he was certain he had seen Horse. He was still trying to wrap his mind around the concept when Nathan spoke again.

"I think he's mad I got him killed."

"Nathan, you did not kill Horse. You loved him. I would even go so far as to say you gave him the happiest eighteen months of his life."

"But he's still dead."

Andrew took Nathan's head between his hands, looking up at him. "He's dead because the processing plant let rat poison get mixed in with the grain. Horse was not the only animal who died as a result. A lot of other people out there right now are grieving horses and ponies."

"But it wouldn't have happened if… I hadn't…"

"It's not your fault."

Andrew found himself wishing the plant still existed so he could sue it again for emotional trauma. He hated seeing Nathan like this, looking defeated and sad. The lightning flickered once more, and this time, there was thunder. The storm was moving closer. Once more, Andrew swore he saw the shaggy form of a great horse in the paddock, tail blowing listlessly in the hot wind.

"Then why is he still out there?" asked Nathan.

He's not out there because there are no such things as ghosts. Andrew gently pulled Nathan's long auburn hair. "Maybe he's worried about you blaming yourself."

"I shouldn't have told him. I'm never telling anything ever again." He looked at Andrew and said quietly, "Especially not you."

Andrew smiled. "I suppose I can live with that."

"Yeah, well… that's kind of the idea."

The rain started to fall. Nathan edged closer to Andrew and kissed him.

"I would like you to stay the night. I'm just… y'know… not sure it's a good idea."

"Well, why don't we try it anyway?"

"And what if you end up… uh… standing in that paddock, staring at me?"

"It won't happen."

The lightning flickered. From the corner of his eye, Andrew swore he caught a brief image of Horse prowling the edges of the paddock.

"You think he really is worried?" asked Nathan. "Not angry?"

"Yes. I do. And I think once you forgive yourself, then… he'll go on."

"Think he might… like… come back and visit?"

"If you want him to."

The thunder boomed quietly. Nathan turned from the window to face Andrew, drawing him close.

"What do I do if…?"

"I die?"

"Yeah."

"Nothing. There are contingencies in place. Believe me, Nathan, I have done everything I can to make certain that you and the boys are protected. Whether I am alive or dead, no one will be able to hurt you."

"That's not what I meant."

"Oh." Andrew stroked the long black hair. "Well… I suppose that's really up to you. Personally, I would like to see you go on and enjoy life. And even if I do spend the night, and for some reason drop dead, it's still not your fault. Okay?"

Nathan didn't look convinced but nodded. "I guess… I should… maybe think about leaving this room."

"Well, it's either that or let Adalwolf take over vocals."

Nathan smiled slightly. He stroked his hand over Andrew's hair. He seemed to ponder something, then finally asked, "Would you… *want*… to spend the night?"

"I would l…"

Nathan raised a hand to Andrew lips, stopping the word. Andrew smiled and lightly bit the finger.

"I mean, I would absolutely hate it."

"Good. 'Cause I'd hate it, too."

Nathan kissed him gently and began slowly undressing him. They fell back to the huge bed, peeling off the rest of their clothes and slipping under the covers. Nathan drew Andrew close and kissed him, trailing his large hands over his small, powerful body.

"Where do you get all these muscles from?"

"Mail order."

Nathan paused and thought about that. Andrew sighed, then laughed.

"I work out twice a day. I'm up every morning at six, before you are even breathing."

"On purpose?"

"Well, it's the only time I have when I don't have other things to do."

"That's harsh. Couldn't you like… change the schedule?"

"Now why would I do that?"

"Well… maybe I could join you."

"Well, here's a thought. How about if you join me in the evening, after dinner?"

"I could do that." Nathan ran his hand over Andrew's hair. "Y'know, you should grow your hair out, put it in a ponytail. You'd be cute… er."

"You think? Maybe I will."

Nathan kissed him, then admitted quietly, "I did write one song. But… I don't think I'll show it to anyone."

"Why not?"

"Well… uh… it's… not my usual style. It's about Horse."

"Well, you don't have to show it to anyone. It was probably catharsis."

"No, actually, it was pretty good."

Andrew grinned. "I mean you were probably venting your feelings."

"Oh. Yeah, I guess I was. I might show someone. Someday. I don't know yet."

"It's up to you."

"Yeah. Well. I'll think about it."

Nathan kissed him, ending the conversation. Outside, the rain fell gently, washing the dry summer dust from the air, sweetening it. The thunder rumbled quietly without threat. Nathan slowly nibbled and kissed and licked his way down Andrew's body.

"I'm glad you're staying. You're just so fucking cute when you're ready to… you know. Like you don't know what to do with yourself."

"I usually don't. I'm a bit of a control freak." Andrew jumped as a warm, wet tongue slowly explored him.

"I hadn't noticed," said Nathan. "I mean… apart from the way you… like… obsessively lace your shoes or line up your pens so they all face due east."

"Nathan, are you being smart with me?"

"I doubt it." He moved up to lie over top of his lover, kissing him softly, then toying with his hair. Andrew draped his arms around his neck.

"So do you hate me?" Andrew asked.

"Yeah. I… really hope you hate me, too. At least enough to put with my crap."

"So long as you don't make me sleep alone anymore."

"No. I won't. I just… couldn't risk… I mean, I'm still not sure this is a good idea." Nathan lowered his head and kissed him. "But not having you here… I didn't like it. And I didn't like knowing you were hurt. I don't want to hurt you." He trailed his hand over Andrew's cheek. "Are you sure I didn't kill Horse?"

"Positive."

"Well, I still don't think I'll risk… saying… that."

"You don't have to tell me. You can just… show me."

"Yeah," said Nathan quietly. "I think I can do that."

He kissed him gently, and a peace settled over the room, broken only by the quiet sounds of lovemaking. Outside, the storm continued to dampen the earth, the rain tapping against the partly-open window, dripping down onto the sill. Down in the paddock, a great shape stared up at the window for a while, then turned and walked into the closed stall and did not return.

ABOUT THE AUTHOR

Alyx Jae Shaw is a writer of sci-fi, fantasy, and horror for a primarily LGBTQT+ audience. Her current (and in her own opinion, BEST work), is Gryphons, which can be found on Amazon, and was attacked by a right wing hate group for reasons that cannot be determined, as they had clearly never read it. She lives in Abbotsford British Columbia with her two pet chickens. It is believed the chickens write the novels themselves using Alyx as a mind-controlled meat-bag. Alyx is fond of cooking, mead-making, drawing, and painting, and talks a lot of smack for someone who once lost an entire unopened can of paint in a small apartment.

https://www.facebook.com/alyx.j.shaw